Praise for MASKMAKER:

*"Extremely well-written, highly inventive,
with really funny jokes"*
Eva Ibbotson

*"Johnson's deft balancing of magic and reality works
perfectly for eight to eleven-year-olds"*
SUNDAY TELEGRAPH

*"A super story . . . If you like your fantasy grounded in
the real world, with real people who happen to get
involved in the forces of magic, then you'll like this . . .
A terrific read, with beautifully drawn descriptive
passages and lots of humour"*
SCHOOL LIBRARIAN

*"There's magic deep in the heart of this highly
inventive story . . . An action-packed adventure
exploding with magic and mystery"*
Julia Eccleshare, LOVEREADING4KIDS.CO.UK

*"Entertaining and thrilling . . . an exciting and
thoroughly enjoyable adventure story"*
BOOKZONE4BOYS.BLOGSPOT.COM

JANE JOHNSON is a writer – for adults and for children – and also works remotely as Fiction Publishing Director for HarperCollins Publishers UK.

For many years she was responsible for the publishing of the works of J.R.R. Tolkien, and as Jude Fisher she wrote the bestselling Visual Companions which accompanied Peter Jackson's movie trilogy of *The Lord of the Rings*.

She is also a trained lecturer and holds a Master's degree in Old Icelandic. When not writing and publishing, she likes to rock climb, and it was in 2005, while researching a novel and climbing in Morocco, that she met her husband: now they split their time between the UK and Morocco, and share their life with Jane's Norwegian Forest Cat, Thorfinna Hairy-Trousers: or Finn, for short.

Also by Jane Johnson

Maskmaker

The Secret Country
The Shadow World
Dragon's Fire

GOLD SEEKERS

JANE JOHNSON

MARION LLOYD BOOKS

First published in the UK in 2011 by Marion Lloyd Books
An imprint of Scholastic Children's Books
Euston House, 24 Eversholt Street
London, NW1 1DB UK
A division of Scholastic Ltd
Registered office: Westfield Road, Southam, Warwickshire, CV47 0RA
SCHOLASTIC and associated logos are trademarks and/or registered
trademarks of Scholastic Inc.

ISBN: 978 1407 10688 5

A CIP catalogue record for this book is available
from the British Library.

Printed by CPI Bookmarque Ltd, Croydon, Surrey
Papers used by Scholastic Children's Books are made from
wood grown in sustainable forests.

1 3 5 7 9 10 8 6 4 2

www.scholastic.co.uk/zone

For William and Yasmin

CONTENTS

THE FINDER

My name is Jude Lanyon and I was born in Cornwall in the year in which they cut the head off a king and turned the natural order of the world upside down.

My father objected that Jude was the patron saint of lost things and not a fair name to give a lad, but my mother reasoned that if Jude was the patron saint of the lost then it must be because he was able to find. "Besides, I've seen his future. The boy is destined to be a finder, and a rich man. Giving him what others consider an ill-fated name will balance matters nicely and save him from envy."

My father smiled and shrugged: her claim sounded outlandish, but he knew his wife was no ordinary woman. When I was seven, our neighbour Susan Tamblin told me that she was a witch. She said it quietly, her eyes as round as platters, and I could tell she believed the gossip. I laughed at her, but when I went home that night and asked Mam outright, she pursed her lips.

"I prefer to be called a wise woman," she said. "I do nothing that would do harm to another living being."

She could tell the coming weather by the shadows in the grass, and cure ailments with poultices and potions. She would often sit silently of an evening with a bowl of water from the stream above the cottage balanced on the table in front of her, looking into its still depths for hours. Then she would pronounce, "Zebedee Rowse will win the wrestling contest in Truro," or "Mary Jago's baby will be a boy." Sometimes she would frown and put the bowl aside with a sigh. She would go outside into our little kitchen-garden and pick herbs and plants and spend hours making tinctures. Then she would gather up her knapsack and set off into the darkness, staff in hand, and go straight to the door of the person who had fallen ill, the person she had scried by magic in the water. How many lives she saved like this in our corner of Cornwall I do not know, but the mere mention of the name of Constance Lanyon had the power to bring a smile to the lips of people from Land's End to Helston town.

She had many other ways of seeing the future: she could read it in the lines on a person's hand or in the patterns made by the leaves in the bottom of a cup of tea, a new luxury from the East that had yet to find favour even among the aristocrats of our country, let alone poor country folk like us. We were far from rich and we had not bought the tea; and thereby hangs a tale.

The night the East India Company brigantine called the *Lady Catherine* was wrecked on the rocks of Cape Cornwall we were waiting for it, along with our neighbours. Mam had "seen" the ship come to grief in a dream, and spied through the clouds that roiled above the sea the sliver of moon that showed her the exact day of the month this event would take place. As the wind howled and the storm battered the shore we pulled the sailors from the waves, some alive and some dead, or as good as, though there were some who muttered that to save them was to draw the Devil's curse, for stealing a soul that was promised to him. The cargo came rolling in on the breakers: great wooden chests that were smashed and splintered on the rocks; bales of coloured fabrics that all came out of the water looking black. Only a couple of chests survived the storm, and inside those there were jars of tea and great pots of pepper and spice. The locals were not greatly interested in the tea (they did not know what it was), but the pepper and spices could be sold in the markets, and cloth was always of use, once you'd dried it out.

This incident served to reinforce my mother's reputation for uncanny knowledge. But what no one outside our family knew was that it was not only spoiled silk and waterlogged goods that we had found. Drawn by an urge I could not explain, or even describe except to say that the palms of my hands itched and my nose twitched like a dog that had scented sausages that might be stolen, I had waded into the crashing surf. I stood there for a moment, sneezing violently, then reached down and laid hands on a small, oblong object. It was heavy: I fairly staggered under the weight of it. I stood there with the sea sucking at my knees, gazing down at my find. It was a small wooden lockbox, very beautifully made, its carvings inlaid with some shiny white stuff that picked up the moonlight.

I went running back to Da and showed it to him. He gave a low whistle, then took the box from me. I saw how surprised he was by its weight: he almost dropped it. Then he wrapped some of the cloth around it and bent his head down close to mine. "This is just the sort of box someone would keep treasure in," he whispered, and put a finger to his lips.

The walk back up the cliff seemed to take an age. I could not wait to get back to our cottage and open the box. As soon as we were there, Da lit the lantern and set the box down on the table and we all gathered around it.

"That's ivory, that is," Mam said, tracing a long finger over the white patterns.

I watched the passage of her finger and saw that the decorations were of animals, animals for which I had no name. They had long, long noses which stretched out and wrapped themselves around the tail of the animal in front, so that they walked in a linked line. I thought they were wonderful.

Da said they were "elephants". It was not a word I knew, but somehow it conjured up exotic foreign places to me. "Where do elephants come from, Da?" I asked, for as far as I knew there were no such things as elephants in Kernow. Cats and dogs and jackdaws and magpies; horses and cows, sheep and foxes and rabbits and rodents; but no elephants.

He had to admit he did not know, precisely; but Mam dropped me a wink. "Some come from India," she said quietly. "But the ones with really big ears, they come from Africa."

"Open it, Da," I breathed.

But it was locked, and there was no key. Da took out his knife and after some careful effort prised the box open. Within lay a dull brown oilcloth, but inside this were coins – pistoles and ducats, thalers and doubloons, crusados and pieces of eight – some gold, many silver and a few in other metals: all sorts of coins from all over the world, Da declared after some examination.

My parents gazed at each other. "You see," Mam said at last, ruffling my hair. "It may have taken nine years to prove me right, but he's a finder, all right."

2

REMOVING TEMPTATION

We did not use all the gold at once as some others might have done but continued to live a simple life, though Mam might have had a new dress or two out of my finding and Da some better quality tobacco.

"We're saving it for a rainy day," Mam said one day a year or so later, finding me on tiptoe on top of a chair on top of the table with my head among the shadows and spiderwebs in the eaves, viewing the gleaming coins in the bottom of the plain earthenware pot in which they were kept. And when I pointed out that there had been a lot of rain lately she simply gave me a sad look and said, "There will always be harder times than these."

And indeed there were, though not necessarily for our family. When Zealous Brown's house burned down and she lost all she had, a new house was soon being raised and her daughter came around and wept her thanks to Mam. And when one of Farmer Scoble's sons fell beneath the plough and his thigh was cut almost to the bone, somehow the money for a fancy surgeon was found and the leg was saved.

All this time Mam worked the garden and tended to her bees, and baked delicious little cakes coloured gold by the saffron she harvested from the meadow behind the house, and Da kept on at the mine. Da was a tinner, though it was far more than simple tin that he dug out of the mine, or sett, as the Cornish call these little family mines. Tin and pyrite he prised away under the ground; bismuth, antimony and semi-precious stones: jasper and opals, amethysts and garnet; black and white and purple and blood, blood red. Sometimes he brought these pretty stones home in his pockets and my mother used some of the crystals in her craft; the rest he sold secretly to a contact in the village of Market-Jew: secretly, because otherwise he'd have had to account for all his findings and pay dues on them to the landowner.

But we wanted for nothing; and as Mam always said, a house full of love is worth far more than a house full of gold.

Our house was just a cottage, a tiny granite building which nestled in a nameless hollow in the valley of Kenidjack in the far western tip of Kernow. In summer it was a place where bees buzzed in the gorse and foxgloves, where kestrels hovered on warm air currents and foxes lazed in pools of sunshine amongst the fragrant heather. It was a place where a boy could lie in the lee of a standing stone of sun-warmed granite and watch the ships sail past on their way to Oporto and Cadiz, Barbary and Rio de Oro, foreign words overheard in the tall tales of sailors.

Boys like me had lain in just such a spot, watching the sun sparkling on the sea, since the time of the first visitors to British shores. They had watched the Phoenicians sail here from the Levant and the Barbary Coast in search of the tin and copper and gold that was hidden in the rocks beneath my feet. They had seen the Romans come and go, the longships of the Danes snake up the coast to raid and plunder; the Crusaders sailing to distant wars, and traders from Spain and Venice and France heading for the port of Hayle. They would have seen warships, too, and fishing vessels, and pirate ships. The sea may look like a great empty expanse, but it is teeming with life, both above and below the waves.

The June of that year was a hot one, and there came a hotter July. I spent most of the summer running about like an urchin, with dirt on my hands and feet, straw in my hair, my skin growing as brown as a hazelnut. I would climb the hill to listen to the wind keen through the stones of Carn Kenidjack and it was not hard to imagine that unearthly wailing sound as the voices of all those lost souls the Devil was said to have imprisoned in the moorland beneath it – which local people call the Gump – crying out to be saved from the torments of Hell. My mother had told me all manner of tales about the Gump, which perhaps was not wise of her given that I was an impressionable boy. I would creep out at all times of the day and night hoping to catch sight of the knockers and spriggans and other fey folk of which she spoke, and came away disappointed only to have

8

seen leaping rabbits and hares and the occasional snuffling hedgehog.

In comparison with the wilds, the tamer charms of our kitchen-garden did not hold much delight for me and I did little to help with the pulling of weeds, the digging or hoeing, leaving it all for Mam to do, along with all the other myriad chores that must be done to keep a household clean, comfortable and well fed. I gave little thought to how meals appeared on the table or fresh linen in the clothes chest: to me it was as if such things were accomplished more by magic than by hard labour. Neither did I give much thought to my father's work. All I knew was that he left the house at first light dressed in his dark clothes and heavy boots, an old linen cap on his head, a knapsack on his back, a new piece of tallow in his pocket and a pickaxe and shovel over his shoulder. He did not return till the sun was setting, looking dog-tired and more often than not bruised and bloody. Sometimes he carried a kibble of the day's winnings with him; but sometimes the haul was too small to bother bringing home.

I remember peeping in that great leather bucket and seeing nothing but grey lumps, dull and lifeless and not at all like metal. There was no silvery sheen to them as I imagined tin should have. My face must have showed my disappointment, for Da grinned, his teeth white in his earth-smeared face. "It takes an expert to spot the ore amidst the rock." But I was not convinced. It looked like rubbish to me.

Da worked his sett with our cousin William, known as Silver Bill. He was a huge, silent man with a shock of grizzled hair and a beard that came halfway down his barrel chest: no ladies' man, as they say. So we were all surprised when Da came back one night, threw his pickaxe to the ground and told us Bill was to be wed, and that as his bride was a woman of some small means, he would no longer be working the claim. "So it seems from now on I must be both burrow-man and shoveller!" He fixed his eyes upon me. "Unless. . ." He caught me by the arm and turned me round and round. "Quite tall now, aren't you, Jude? And those muscles are developing well enough. Perhaps we should discover what else you have a gift for finding. Maybe you'll prove to have a nose for gold under the ground, as well as in the sea!"

I opened my mouth to cry off, for I had no wish to go down a mine, but it was Mam who came to my rescue. "No, Rob: he's far too young. Let him enjoy his childhood. Heaven knows it lasts too short a time."

They argued into the night and I fell asleep with my hands over my ears. But in the morning it seemed Mam had won, for by the time I got up Da had gone off to the mine on his own. "Must he always be a tinner?" I asked as I ate my breakfast. "If we just used the gold I found he could stop working altogether."

She smiled at me and smoothed my hair out of my eyes. "It's not just about money, Jude. All men must work, and all women too. It's what forms our characters and teaches us

10

the value of things – even of life itself. Have you never noticed how unhappy are the rich and idle?"

I thought about this as I chewed and decided, as usual, that Mam was right. Once I had spied the local lord and his family at a feast day in Market-Jew and their mouths had been downturned with dissatisfaction and their voices raised in complaint despite all their fancy clothes and well-fed, soft pink flesh.

"Your da is a fine man, but gold is a curse," Mam said, climbing up to take the earthenware pot down from the eaves, "and a temptation, even to the best of men."

She emptied the contents on to the table, and it seemed to me that more than half the coins had already gone. Then she looked up at me. "The best course is to remove the temptation." And she scooped the remaining coins into the pocket of her apron and went to the door. There she turned, a finger to her lips. "Don't tell, and don't look, Jude." She went out into the garden, and when she came back a quarter hour later it was with earth under her nails and an empty pocket.

3

PLAGUE

The argument of the night before had left me feeling the world might turn upside down. I felt in need of company. But I had no real friends my own age with whom I might play or chatter: perhaps because my mother was a witch they all kept away from me. But I had friends, of a sort. Old John had once been a sailor and adventurer and he was often to be found sitting outside the Tinner's Arms, cradling a mug of beer between his chest and the stump that replaced the hand he had lost in some long-ago battle. He had a fund of stories that set a boy to dreaming and forgetting the problems in his own life.

Stories about seas filled with speaking whales and mountainous islands inhabited by miniature people. About Barbary raiders with shaved heads and curved swords who sailed into harbours in ships as silent as ghosts, come to steal men for the slave markets in far-away Africa.

Old John was exactly where he usually was: sitting upon an upturned bucket outside the inn, waiting for someone to take pity on him and give him a flagon of ale in exchange for one of the odd things he whittled. He was a wizard with a knife was Old John. Give him a bit of hawthorn and a few minutes and he would transform it into a little lifelike dog or horse, with the knot in the wood for its eye and the grain sweeping up into its tail. That day he was engaged in a whittling contest with one of his odd collection of friends: a foreign sailor I'd seen once or twice before who visited John when he was between voyages. He had nut-brown skin, a ready smile and eyes as black as sloes and I liked him, even though John said he had once been a Barbary pirate. I was sure he was teasing me, for Abdellah was gentle and funny and had no malice to him at all. Nor did he carry a curved sword, though I always kept an eye out for it. Whether he shaved his head, I did not know, for it was always covered by a long piece of cloth he called a "turban".

In no time at all, John had made me a whistle that made cuckoo calls; and Abdellah took a piece of twine from his pocket and wound it around the disc he had carved and showed me how it would dance up and down the string if you flicked it just right. I declared Abdellah the winner, and he grinned from ear to ear. Then they set about telling stories, each one topping the last in fancy. I found Abdellah's accent hard to follow at times – he said he was from Morocco, which sounded very different to Barbary to me. He told stories about magical spirits trapped in bottles ("Oh, I know about those!" Old John declared with a wink), flying carpets and wicked sorcerers, and treasures and talking fishes, and all the sort of things a boy most loves to hear about. He had more disturbing tales, too, of desert sands that could swallow whole armies and leave no trace, of cities made of gold and guarded by dragons, and creatures that could change shape and then disappear like a wisp of smoke. One of these tales was so distressing that I am ashamed to say it made me cry out in terror, at which point Abdellah took a cone of sugar out of his pack, hammered a little piece off it and popped it in my mouth. "To take away nasty taste of the djinn," he said. Old John roared with laughter and said it was not a good thing for a boy my age to be drinking gin anyway.

Then he set about proving he was a better storyteller than the man from Morocco, and told of armadas crewed by skeletons and secret palaces that rose from the waves when the moon was in the right quarter. About mermaids and mermen, and the fish with nine tails.

"And now," he declared, "I will tell you a true tale about a friend of mine called Cannibal Saul." He drew long and deep on his clay pipe. "A man is a curious thing," he said. "When it comes right down to it he is no more than an animal."

He told me how Saul had been cast adrift in the ship's longboat with three of his crewmates off the Azores for some unspecified crime.

"Cast adrift without even a waterskin or the means to catch a fish," he said darkly. "There ain't no act that deserves such punishment."

They had drifted for days under a hot sun, borne along by the currents of the ocean, and became so thirsty they were driven to drink seawater, which merely served to make their condition worse. Their lips cracked; their tongues dried and swelled till they could barely breathe. One by one they had succumbed to madness, then to death. At last only Saul was left.

Old John leaned towards me, licking lips that were gnarled and twisted as a tree root. "I was in the ship what picked him up. Just Saul: that was all there was left in that longboat. Surrounded by the skellingons and gnawed limbs of his crewmates." He left a long gap into which all manner of horrible thoughts came bobbing.

"I can see you've got there afore me, young Jude. He had to eat them, you see, and they ha' done the same."

The marrow in my bones froze. I had nightmares all that summer.

I was so caught up in my own imaginings that I did not even notice when my mother became ill. It was only when she took to her bed and lay down with the blanket over her head and told me at all pains to keep out of the house that I realized all was not well with the world.

My da, though, was most alarmed to come home from the mine, covered in grime and tired to the bone, to find a cold hearth and no supper, and me sitting useless as an owl in daylight by the door, regarding her with big eyes.

"She's sick," I said, though it was all too plain to see.

My da knelt by her side and took her hand. "Send the boy away," was all she said. "Send him to Mrs Scoble, and go there yourself. Promise me."

"I'll not leave you."

"You must. 'Tis the only thing that will give me peace of mind."

"I'll take the boy, then. But I'll be back."

She had to be satisfied with that, though I saw tears well up and escape the closed lids of her eyes and run off down cheeks that were usually rosy but were now as pale as the moon.

"Kiss him for me, for I dare not," she said, looking at me with all her heart in her eyes. And then she turned her face to the wall.

I do not remember much of those next few days. Farmer Scoble and his wife were a kind couple, but they were distracted by their own troubles: a sickly baby and a little girl of seven called Beth whose back had begun to bend in on itself like a hairpin and who cried day and night at the torture of it and was not long for the world, according to Mam. They had half a dozen other children besides — all boys, including the lad whose leg had been saved. I heard the words "plague" and "pestilence", though they were uttered quietly and not meant for my ears; but no one knew for sure what ailed my mother.

When they told me she was dead I did not believe them. She was a wise woman, was she not? She healed sick people all the time: Mistress Tamblin's rheumatics, old Mr

Ellis's ague, John Blewett's case of boils. She even healed animals, wild things that would not usually let a person near them: hares with broken legs, a peregrine with a damaged wing; so how could she not heal herself? There was a lot of muttering to the same effect in the village. The other children stared at me and made comments when they thought I was not listening. Alan Jacka said it was a punishment on her for using magic. I hit him so hard his nose bled. After that they left me alone and I made the best of my own company.

On her funeral day, when they were taking her corpse from the house in a rough-hewn box on William Bolitho's fishcart, someone shouted, "Turn the bees!" There was a great to-do because no one had thought to tell the bees that their mistress was dead, which as everyone knows brings the worst of luck. Molly Ellis picked up her skirts and ran up the meadow and sang to them, "Stay at home, pretty bees, fly not away! Mistress Constance is dead and gone." Then she turned the hives around.

I did not go to the funeral. I hid instead, and then took myself up to the hives. It seemed Molly's song had done the trick, for the bees were all still in there buzzing and chattering away, sharing the news.

I opened a hive and the bees let me take the combs out. They buzzed and buzzed around me, but not a one of them stung me. Liquid gold dripped everywhere, the sunlight striking through it as it fell. I licked my fingers. It was the best honey I had ever tasted and it remains the strongest memory I have of my mother's funeral, though that seems a terrible thing to say.

The summer was to get worse yet, though it hardly seemed possible after the passing of Mam. The signs were all there, for odd things kept happening right through to Lammastide. A pod of whales was washed up on the beach at Cot Valley Cove. No matter what anyone did they could not be saved. Even when the fishers towed them off with ropes into the ocean, they turned right back and kept swimming into the shallows as if they had a will to die. Boats went down under clear skies; people were found walking naked in their sleep, speaking in tongues, and some lost their wits altogether. People said the fey folk had taken them and left walking scarecrows in their stead. And one day Da went wild in the cottage and destroyed almost everything in it.

I came back from one of my jaunts along the cliffs to find him sitting amidst the wreckage, wild-eyed and staring. "The gold," he said hoarsely, "it's gone." The earthenware pot lay smashed in bits on the floor. I stared at it guiltily, but said nothing for fear of his temper.

4

THE MINE

The next morning, Da shook me awake. "Come on, Jude, wake up. Your life of leisure is over."

I gazed at him, sleepy and uncomprehending.

"Put on your canvas trousers and your leather boots, your black wool jacket too. It gets cold down there."

"Down where?" But I already knew what he meant and a chill began to spread through my stomach.

"Without your mam we face hard times," he said, bending to put on his own boots, hulking great things that Mam had never allowed in the house, but which now lived on either side of the fire like two great lurking crows, waiting for some carrion to tear into. "You're a man now and you can work your way."

A man. I was twelve years old. I almost felt my chest swell with pride. But I remembered what it was he wanted me to do. "I don't think I'm cut out to be a tinner, Da," I said quietly.

"Nonsense, Jude, it's in your blood. My da was a tinner, and his da before him, and on and on back to the times of King Arthur and all his knights."

"But I can't go down the mine. I can't even bear to go in a cave!" It was true. Down in the cove there was a split in the rock wall which went back and back into the darkness. Some said it ran all the way to the core of the earth where the wizard Merlin slept in a cave full of crystals and treasures. If you got in there and woke him up he would grant you a wish and make your dreams come true. Oddly, though, no one had managed to get further than twenty feet or so into the cave before being overcome by the chill and terror of the place. This was not surprising to me. I knew I would not like to be disturbed from centuries of rest by some nosy boy. Merlin would surely have set a spell to keep people out, a spell only a greater magician could break. In any case it simply wasn't natural to go into dark holes in the world.

Da's usually mild eyes sharpened with irritation. "Get dressed and say not another word."

He stood and waited for me outside the door, puffing furiously on his pipe.

My feet felt like lead as we tramped across the moor tops to the sett. Da walked with the pickaxe balanced on his shoulder and the cat's head mallet in his hand. I carried a shovel and a knapsack containing a lantern and some hastily gathered food. Before long the furze and bracken gave way to tips of rubble, a wasteland of stones tumbled one on another.

"This is what we call the attle or the deads," Da was saying. "All the useless rock that comes out of the mine so

20

that we may get at the ore. And this reddish, cindery stuff you see around is the gozzans – that's where the old ones used to work. Ah, they knew a thing or two, the old men. It's not an easy thing to find tin-ore, or the rocks that bear it. That takes a nose, that does. It takes a finder. And that's why you're here with me at last, Jude. I'm counting on you!"

He laughed heartily, but I did not feel like laughing. I found myself staring at the big leather bucket hanging from the hoist as if it were a hanged man swaying on a gibbet. Beneath it – a ragged black void amid the piles of rubble and turned earth – was the shaft itself. The cold reality of what I was about to do gripped me then. I stopped dead. "Oh, Da, don't make me go down there!"

But he said nothing and only pushed me ahead of him, made my knapsack secure across my back and handed me down to the wooden ladder built into the black hole. "Set each foot carefully and always keep three points of contact," he told me mercilessly.

"But it's dark, how can I see?"

"You don't need to see to go down a ladder. Just feel with your feet."

"But how will I know when I'm at the right place?"

He laughed. "You'll know."

And after that there was no more arguing and down I went till I was swallowed up by the darkness and the circle of daylight overhead seemed to diminish to no more than a pinprick. I was in pitch-blackness, alone in a silence such as I have never experienced before or after. All I could hear was the beat and rush of blood in my ears. Oh, and it was cold! Now I understood the term "colder than the grave". Yet a grave was only a fathom underground, and I was sure I had passed many fathoms. Then my foot slipped on the polished rung below me and suddenly I was clinging on for dear life, scrabbling for grip like a spider in a washbowl.

At last I got myself back on the ladder and clung to it, my forehead pressed to the cold rock. My heart raced. I felt hot and cold. I was sure I would faint and fall to my death, but somehow I managed to hang on. Then I reached down and stubbed my foot on something more than a rung and a moment later I was no longer on the ladder but on solid ground, and realized that my great drama, my near-fall, had taken place no more than three feet off the floor of the mine shaft. I felt a fool.

"Are you down, Jude?"

Da's voice seemed a thousand miles away.

"I'm down!" I called back. My cry echoed off the walls of the shaft till it sounded as if there were twenty Judes in the pit.

In my knapsack I had a candle-lantern and a flint. With shaking hands I lit the candle, reasoning that if I could see where I was I would not be so frightened. How wrong I was. The flickering light showed me the smallness of the space. The shaft was narrower than the span of my arms, and where I now crouched with the lantern two tunnels led off in different directions. One was large enough that a man might walk through it with his head bowed low, but the other seemed too small for even a child to crawl through. This one dipped steeply away so that the light of the lantern barely illuminated it beyond the first two or three feet.

Despite my thick jacket and sturdy boots I started to quake and shiver. I was sure Da had brought me down here to send me into the little tunnel. The idea was frightful to me, for the very idea of being underground was horror enough, let alone to be sent into what looked hardly larger than a rabbit hole. I started to sneeze violently.

"Caught a cold, have you, lad?" Da asked, his boots thumping on to the ground beside me. He set the great kibble down and shook his head. "Better set you to work. That'll soon warm you up!"

"Don't send me down there," I begged, backing away from the smaller tunnel. "Please, Da."

"There? That's the adit, boy. Don't you know anything?" And he explained to me how every mine needed a channel that would drain the water away out of it, and that this was the purpose of the small tunnel. "It comes out in the cliffside and the water pours directly into the sea," he said proudly.

All the way to the cliff's edge. The idea of this made me shiver even harder. I could not imagine how men as large as my father or Silver Bill could have made such a long, narrow tunnel.

Now Da pushed me ahead of him into the main level.

"The lode's down here," he told me. "It's nearly worked out, but before I start digging out another drift I want to be sure there's no more to be had from it. So down you go, Jude, right to the end, and see what you can find."

That was a hard day, the hardest day of my life. While Da inserted wedges into the rocks and pounded at them with the mallet, I gathered the waste rock and loaded it into the bucket and dragged it back up the level to the shaft, where I attached it to the rope, then climbed the ladder to the surface and wound the bucket up on the winch. Then I emptied the kibble on to the spoil heap and lowered it down the shaft again before climbing back down the ladder into the darkness. Each time I came up into the light all I wanted to do was to take to my heels and run along the clifftops as far and as fast as I could. But something — conscience or duty, or simple fear — kept me at my task all that long day. By the end of it, though, there seemed precious little to show for all our hard work: just a few meagre lumps of grey-black ore which barely half-filled the bucket. I sat, exhausted, at the foot of the ladder, trying to summon the energy to climb it for the last time. My hands were hot and itchy, no doubt from the scratchy hemp rope to which I had attached the kibble, and my nose was prickling. Then a great sneeze escaped me. And another and another. I felt myself irresistibly drawn towards the drainage channel; and the next thing I knew I found myself crawling along it like a moldywarp.

Something caught me by the ankle and I cried out in

terror. Worse, I found the tunnel was so tight around me that I could not turn to face my attacker. I lay there in the freezing dark and cold with water seeping up through my breeches and coat, and then I was hauled swiftly backwards.

"What in the world were you thinking, Jude, to crawl down the adit?"

Da was shaking his head. In the light of the candle-lantern I bowed my head and saw that I was now covered from head to foot in thick black mud. Now I even looked like a moldywarp. Or a knocker, the little black creatures of Cornish legend, which toil in the earth seeking their own lodes of metal. "I . . . I don't know. It just . . . happened."

He caught me by the arms and gazed at me intently. There was a new light in his eye. "Did you see something? Does the lode continue in that direction? Or perhaps you came upon something else?"

In response, all I could do was sneeze and scratch my palms. The burning sensation in my head was becoming unbearable, and I knew the only thing that would assuage it was to go into the adit.

"Give me the lantern." Before I could consider the wisdom of my actions I was crawling through the little tunnel once more. Now that I could see, it was even more terrifying, for the slope dropped sharply away ahead of me. What would happen if I slipped? Would I slide all the way down the adit and spew out of the end like the drainage water, and into the crashing sea below? Maybe the tide

25

would be out and I would smash to my death upon the rocks. . . But even that thought could not stop me. Something had hold of me in quite a different way to the grip Da had had on my ankle, and its pull was even stronger. I shone the lantern and something winked in the candlelight. I took out my pocket knife and scratched at the surface, and four sparkling grains fell into my outstretched hand.

"'Tis gold!" Da cried when he examined my find, but it was no surprise to me. I had known it from the moment my nose began to prickle. He sent me back in with the iron pick. "Leave it by the lode, lad. It'll keep the knockers away."

I thought he had gone quite mad with the discovery, but I did what he told me. All the way back home he talked and talked. The plans he had! He would enlarge the adit by using quicklime to break the rock, and because I had made the find he would teach me how to set it, but first he would have to show me how to make a borehole and to ram it tightly with clay stemming. . .

By now I had stopped listening. My heart was heavy. I had made a rod for my own back by finding the gold, and now it would be used to beat me. I would have to go back down that accursed hole, day in, day out, until the gold was worked out.

But it did not happen quite like this, though I wish it had. I spent only two days back in the sett, taking turns with Da drilling in the little adit till my arms burned and my head throbbed with the effort and the grinding noise. If it was uncomfortable for me, it must have been terrible for him, for he was twice my size, but he made not a single murmur of complaint. The promise of the gold was perhaps too great, or he simply did not feel the horror I felt at being so tightly enclosed. At last we managed to bore a hole the length of my hand. Now came the lime. Da looked at me dubiously. "I will do this," he said at last. "Lime burns easily, and with the water coming down the adit it's too dangerous for you, Jude." He explained to me how when lime and water come together it burned worse than fire, and how it was this heat that would break the rocks apart so that he could extract the gold.

Back in he went and set the quicklime; then, very quickly, I saw the soles of his boots advancing towards me as he reversed out of the tunnel.

"Up the ladder, Jude. Up you go."

I needed no second encouragement. Up I went, with Da close behind. If I was expecting an explosion I was to be disappointed, for there was so sound at all. Da saw my face and smiled. "We'll check the results tomorrow. Poisonous fumes."

The next day he could not wait to get back to the adit and examine the lode. But when we got there it was to find the quicklime had had precious little effect. Da was in a black mood all day. That night he went to the Tinner's Arms and did not return until I was abed.

The next morning he was up early but when I dragged myself to the table, he shook his head. "Not today, Jude. Today you have the freedom of the wide world." He took a little leather pouch from his pocket and weighed it in his hand. Its dusty, musky smell wafted into my nose, and for one desperate moment I thought I might sneeze and send it everywhere.

"What's in it, Da?"

"This, lad, is black powder."

I frowned. "The stuff they use to fire a cannon?"

"The very same. If quicklime won't do it then gunpowder surely will. I got it from a man down at the market, an old, one-eyed veteran of the wars. He swore it was the best quality. I'll set the powder in the same bore and lay some straw to take the fire to it. But this is man's work, not for a boy. Tomorrow we'll reap the rewards. Go play, Jude. Make the most of this glorious weather."

It was a beautiful day. I spent much of it lazing in the sun-browned furze watching the long, slow shadows of basking sharks slide past in the turquoise waters beneath Roscommon. I was wandering happily along the tops when there came a great, deep, low rumble, far away, yet close at hand. And with it came a trembling underfoot, so that I thought my knees were giving way. But then I saw the heads on the sea pinks nodding and bobbing with the vibration, and all around birds that had been roosting peaceably on the turf suddenly took to the air with a clatter of wings. After that all was quiet again.

I knew without a shadow of doubt what had happened. Taking to my heels, I ran like the wind towards Da's sett, my feet slapping hard on the earth. The idea of my da trapped down there in the darkness, beneath a fall of rock, was a thought so awful to me that it chased all my fears of the dark tunnels away. I would go down the adit myself, so I would, I would tear the granite away with my bare hands to free him!

But when I got near the sett I could tell without even looking that there was nothing I could do. Gone was the winch and the neat little shaft-hole beneath it. Instead there was a great ragged crater in the ground, and all was unearthly silent.

5

ORPHAN

I took off running and could not stop. I ran and ran with tears blinding my eyes so I could not see where I was going. I ran across the moor and up the lane, past the hawk-trees that reached their gnarled arms out to try to catch me, past the people running to discover the cause of the blast. I ran past the gate that led to the cottage but I did not go home. I could not stand the idea of the place being so empty. So I just kept on running.

It was Farmer Scoble who found me the next morning, curled up in the straw in his barn with the farm cats pressed up against me as if we were all of the same litter.

"What's this, young 'un?" he said, while I blinked my eyes and stared at his thick silhouette. "What are you doing here, of all places?"

For a time I didn't know where "here" was, for I was still caught in the toils of a dream in which I was out on the cliffs, lying with my cheek pressed into the heather, listening to an explosion down in the depths of the earth, an explosion that went on and on and on, at the heart of which my da screamed and wailed like a lost soul, cursing me for sending him to his death. At the same time I heard my mother's voice pronouncing over and over: "Gold is a curse and a temptation."

Now I sat up and saw where I was. My heart was still beating too fast and there was a sweat on my face. Or perhaps it was that one of the chets, the new kittens, had licked me, mistaking me for their mother. One of them had crawled into the pocket of my smock and twisted now to regard me with reproach as if to say, "What did you move for? I was sound asleep." It was a rough little thing, neither one colour nor another, but a patchwork of black and dirty white, as if it were the product of two different fathers, which can be the way with cats sometimes.

Two fathers, and I none at all. Quite suddenly and with a shock of memory I felt tears start to my eyes. First Mam, now Da: what cruelty there was in the world! A great sob rose up and escaped me, and then the tears came splashing out. I dashed them away fiercely, aware that Farmer Scoble, who was so hard of demeanour and strong of arm, was staring at me. I might be only twelve, but now I had to be a man, for I was all that was left of our little family.

"I . . . I could not go home," I managed to get out, clenching my teeth against the misery.

He looked embarrassed. "Aye, 'tis a shame. Your da was a good man. Ar, well, young 'un, come indoors with me." So there it was, the confirmation of his death, of which I knew I was the cause.

I followed him like a stray dog into the farmhouse kitchen, where his wife and her various infants regarded me with large eyes. The baby was wailing in its crib, and the next oldest was wailing too. I felt sure I would be the next to add to the hullabaloo, especially when Mother Scoble folded me into her large bosom so that I could hardly breathe. "Poor lad, poor little orphan."

An orphan. That was what I was. I had not even thought of the word. It rolled around my head, becoming a nonsense. *An orphan, an orphan, a norphan. . .*

She released me and the children made way on the bench on which they were squeezed. One of the older ones – Henry, I think his name was – took the next child on to his knee so that I might sit down. They all stared at me. I stared at the table, not used to such a crowd. There wasn't much to see: just the bare boards and a few crumbs; a half-eaten bowl of some greyish porridge with a wooden spoon sticking up out of it like a waymarker. Mother Scoble pushed this towards me. "There, Jude, you eat that and you'll feel better."

One of the other children now started to wail at the loss of its breakfast, but even before this I knew I could not eat it. There was too hard a lump in my throat and barely room for words to pass, let alone porridge.

The farmer and his wife went into the other room and started talking in low voices. Although I was out of sight, I could still hear every word they said.

"Poor little lamb," said Mistress Scoble. "All alone in the world."

"We cannot give him a roof for more than a few nights: there are already too many mouths to feed."

"Is there no work on the farm he might do for his keep?"

"If he could pull a plough he might be useful come the spring now that Henry can't do it; but he's a scrawny little fellow, and only likely to get scrawnier eating our scraps."

"If only he were a girl. I could do with some help around the house."

Crying infants drowned out the next exchange, as if even the little ones wanted to make their feelings on the subject heard. The next words I caught were "aunt in Penzance", and I can tell you, that made my ears prick up and another sort of panic rise.

It was true, I did have an aunt in Penzance. Her name was Piety, or Po-Face, or some such Puritan thing. Da liked to jibe at Mam that her sister was a Bible-basher. I could just imagine her swiping me over the head with a heavy great family Bible, for when I had met her she had made a thoroughly disagreeable impression on me. She wore a tall black hat and had a nose so sharp it looked as if it could poke its way into anyone's business and out the other side. After taking one look at me, she had sniffed through that snooty beak and chided my mother, "Constance, have you no pride at all? It is bad enough that you should abandon the true way of the Lord and marry a low miner without our poor dear father's permission, but that you have raised the boy like a savage brings shame on our family name! Look at him, with his skin as dark as a Spaniard's and his hair as shaggy as a pony's. Leave him with me for a week or two and I shall scrub and beat some manners into him."

I would not go to the aunt in Penzance, I thought fiercely, even though it would be a fit punishment for finding the gold that had driven Da to his death. But then I heard a worse thing. I only caught the tail end of it, but it sent a shiver down my spine, and not just the words, but also for the low, quiet way in which it was said: "*beadle*" and then ". . .*workhouse in Bodmin*. . ."

The beadle was the parish officer, I knew that much, and not a man to cross. Bodmin was the place where the mad people lived, a town far to the east of Kernow, up above the moors. The conjunction of that with the idea of a "workhouse" sounded very bad indeed.

Perhaps they sensed that I was listening, for the farmer and his wife came back in, looking distinctly shifty.

"You can stay with us till after your father's funeral," Farmer Scoble told me. "How's that for now?"

"I don't want to go to the workhouse!" I cried hotly, and watched them exchange an embarrassed glance.

"What long ears you do have," Mother Scoble said, blushing. "There, there, you shan't go to the workhouse, I'm sure. They don't send children to the workhouse if they have family willing to take them in. John's going to seek out your relatives in Penzance. Something good will surely come of it."

I bit back any objection to being sent to my aunt. If I made a noise about that, then the workhouse it would be.

The memorial service, it turned out, was set for three days hence, and so three days of liberty I would have here at the farm. As a boy you are never able to think far ahead. Three days seemed an eternity, and I was still stunned with the shock of my circumstances. I took myself off to the barn to commiserate with the cats and try not to think about Mam and Da and what might become of me. I was still there at dinner time when Henry, the second eldest boy, came and found me lining the chets up in order of size and weight, addressing them by make-believe names and instructing them in the chores I expected them to do around our non-existent house and garden. When he said my name, I fair leapt a mile.

"What are you doing?"

He was a plain boy with a big doughy face and small dark eyes that seemed almost lost in it, but his gaze was uncomfortably penetrating, and I never once saw him smile.

"Nothing," I said defensively, though it was clear that no natural cats would line themselves up in a straight line so.

He just kept staring at me and then asked, "What's it like being an orphan?"

I had very successfully not thought about this for the last couple of hours but his solemn regard struck me to the core, and suddenly the tears came welling up again and spilled and spilled and spilled.

He stared at me in dismay, maybe having never seen another boy weep before, but I could not stop. Even the cats watched me curiously, as well they might, with the snot running out of my nose.

"I come to tell you there's stew," he announced, and ran back to the house.

I had eaten nothing for the whole of a day, I realized, as the pangs clawed suddenly at my insides. Children are resilient beasts. I am ashamed to say I dried my face on the straw and went inside and wolfed down two bowls of Mother Scoble's good stew.

6

THE CHET

I slept that night in the barn, preferring my own company and that of the kittens to the brood of Scobles. When I say I slept, rather I lay there in the straw for a long time, trying not to think, listening to the cows shuffle and low in the byre and the rats scuttling along the beams, waiting for the sun to come up and chase off the darkness. When at last the dawn brightened the air I filched an apple from the barrel in the corner of the barn and ate it down, wondering all the while what to do with myself now that I was an orphan.

Now I had an idea of what happened to orphans and the destitute, an idea became fixed in my head. The beadle would come for me and send me to the workhouse, in Bodmin town, that place full of mad people, for I would not go to the horrid aunt in Penzance. And so I determined to run away and seek my own fortune. Since Mam had said it would be considerable, I knew nothing truly bad could happen to me. But there were things I would need from our house. I crept out of the barn.

I was about to climb over the hedge overlooking our land when I saw two men in sombre coats and hats such as parish men wear appear at the top of the lane. I watched them make their way over the field and down through the kitchen-garden that had been Mam's pride and joy. They knocked upon the door of our house as if there were gentlefolk within who might bid them enter. When there was no answer, they unlatched the door and went in, and came out again after a scant minute. Then I knew it was me they were looking for, for there was no good reason to come out again so fast except that it was clear there was nowhere within even for a small boy to hide. My heart beat as quick and light as a bird's as I watched them search the outhouse. The kitten in my pocket (where it seemed to have taken up residence), perhaps sensing my disquiet, butted its head against my chest and purred so loudly I almost cried aloud.

When the seekers had gone, I got to my feet and made to climb the hedge, but the kitten dug its claws into my skin and miaowed piteously. "What, would you throw in your lot with me?" I asked it, and it turned its head up to me, regarding me with a pair of eyes as bright as lamps. Then it juggled something up and out on to the ground. I kept a number of objects in the pocket of my smock: a small knife, a shell in which you could hear the sea shooshing back and forth, a whistle fashioned from a hollow stick that set dogs to barking, and a lodestone that my mother had given me. "Now you will always know which way is north," she told me, as if to know this was a useful thing. It was the lodestone on its string that the kitten had pushed out of my pocket.

The lodestone was a mysterious object. It had started life as a piece of heavy ore my father had brought out of the sett one day and given to Mam, since he knew it would be useful to her in her craft. She had by some means bored a hole in it (though how I knew not, for it was as dense as lead) and threaded a cord through it. When dangled on its string, the stone would swing and twist until at last it set itself rocking clearly in one direction. Always the same direction, my mother showed me, as if it knew where it wanted to go.

I picked it up now and let it swing, and sure enough it showed me what I already knew, that north of me lay the cliffs and then the sea. No help, that. Kernow is set about on three sides with water, and yet I had never so much as set foot in a boat, nor ever been into the sea above my knees. I feared the way it sucked and dragged at the beach, and the noise of the rocks and pebbles trying and failing to resist it, and I could not – or would not – swim.

North and south and west lay sea; and east lay . . . Bodmin, and the world beyond where they spoke none of our language. What to do? I pondered this long and hard, watching the lodestone swing its steady course, until the kitten leapt down from my pocket and batted the stone like a plaything and then set off, trotting, as if it had made my decision for me.

*

It felt strange entering the house I had lived in for all my twelve years. I did so furtively, like a thief, meaning to leave it with possessions that were not my own. I could no longer call it my home, for it takes people to make a house a home, and not merely walls and a roof. Empty of its occupants, and with no possibility of their coming back, it felt a sad and lonely place indeed, with cold cinders in the fireplace and the leavings of the last meal Da and I took together still on the bare board of the table. The bread, when I touched it, was hard as stone. The bit of yellow cheese that sat beside it had cracked and dried. But I ate it anyway and gave some to the chet as well, who ate it enthusiastically with the side of his mouth, growling in warning all the time in case any might try to separate him from his prize.

I gathered a few things I thought I might have need of and went out into the sunshine as quickly as I could. The house made me uneasy, as if it was angry at its abandonment. Or perhaps the parish men had affronted it by making some remark about the meanness of its few rooms, its bare stone floors and rough-hewn furniture.

Outside I picked and ate what I could in the kitchen-garden. There were some strawberries and loganberries and a near-ripe plum or two. I pocketed a few half-grown apples and some hard pears. The gooseberries I left where they grew, guarded by their thorns and their hairy skins. I had never much liked them even when Mam cooked them up with a bit of honey.

Honey. . .

No one had told the bees that now Da had gone as well as Mam. I looked to the hives. Did it matter whether the bees flew or stayed where there was no one left to gather the product of their industry? I decided it was a matter of politeness to inform them at least. Bees are wise creatures and Mam had always taught me to respect them. "Be gentle with a bee," she told me when one day I had tried to swat one away, thinking it a good-for-nothing wasp, "for it will pay you back a thousandfold for your kindness, and their gold has brought more good into the world than any amount of that yellow ore sitting down in the ground, calling for greedy men to come and dig it out."

I tramped up through the meadow to the hives and turned them till they faced south, towards the open fields. "Your master has followed your mistress," I told them with a catch in my voice. "So you must choose whether you go or stay."

They did not reply, of course.

But my hands began to itch uncontrollably, and the palms began to burn. Then it was as if a mist descended on me, for the next thing I knew I was kneeling on the ground with a small pile of coins before me and dirt beneath my nails. So, this had been Mam's hiding place for the gold! Now I had grubbed it up, but too late to help my poor Da. I stashed the coins away in my pack, feeling as guilty as a thief all the while. But the bees did not seem to blame me for my theft, for when I reached the top of the lane and looked back they were issuing out of the hives like a great black funeral ribbon, heading for the open moors.

41

UNCLE MOMO

It was past the middle of the afternoon before I found myself standing on Watch Hill. I could see in every direction. The blue sea sparkled at my back, to my right, and ahead, like a shimmering cloth where the sun touched it, and all the hills were clothed in flowers and purple heather. The heat of the sun had brought all sorts of colours into the landscape and I thought as I walked along how much Mam would have loved to see all the bright things in the hedges – the white trumpets of the columbines, the golden glow of the buttercups and the last of the towering foxgloves and all the other flowers for which I had no name, but which she had known as well as her own hand. Then I felt the loss of her all over again, and the knowledge that poor Da lay in a dark place all crushed and broken, and then I am ashamed to say that despite the lovely scenery and the joyous flight of the rooks and starlings over the moor, I could not help but weep like a girl again.

How long I stood there, punishing my leaking eyes with my hands, I do not know, but the next thing I knew the kitten had climbed out of my pocket, and digging its little claws into my smock, and more particularly, into my skin, made its way precipitously and head first to the ground by way of my chest, hip and leg. It sat there, mewing, as if to say, "Stop that, and pay attention!"

Its gaze was uncomfortably direct. I had the distinct feeling it was trying to tell me something, but I was just a boy and had none of my mother's magic and so its mewing just sounded like "Miaow, miaow, miaowww!" I bent to pick it up and restore it to my pocket, but it skipped away from me a little distance and then set up its noise again.

"What do you want?" I asked it crossly, for I knew the answer was probably "something to eat". And unless cats had taken to eating fruit, then there was nothing I could offer it.

In answer, the chet climbed on to a rock and sat there, eyeing me hard. I sighed and shook my head. "I do not know what you want. If we are to be anywhere I can find you a fish head or two for your supper then we had best move on!"

So we walked all that long afternoon, down lanes thick with ferns and brambles in which the ripening berries glowed like little rubies, over wooden stiles, across fields deep with emerald grass, or bitten down to the quick by sheep and studded with rabbit holes. We passed standing stones which stood like sentinels peering out over the landscape, and circles that looked as if a giant had set up a game of skittles and then wandered away and forgotten

43

about it. We passed cows grazing so contentedly they barely lifted their heads to take notice of a ragged boy with a bag slung over his back and a kitten in his pocket. Once a cart passed us by, but it was laden with spuds and turnips still with fresh earth on them and the carter did not stop to offer us a ride, but gave us a wide berth and clicked his tongue to encourage his nag to go faster.

The sun was beginning to dip by the time we toiled up the hill towards Castle an Dinas. I remembered Da saying this place had once been the fortress of a tribal chief. It did not look much like a fortress now. Great runners of ivy and tumbles of bramble had colonized the earth ramparts and blurred their outlines. The kitten took a little water from my father's old leather flask as I sat there, seeing in my mind's eye a fierce-looking man with fiery red hair like Mam's, all in knots and braids, even down to his long moustaches, wearing a robe of gold and black Cornish plaid over stoutly muscled limbs, a greatsword strapped to his side, and eyes as bright as periwinkles and as sharp as a peregrine falcon's. He would have seen invaders coming for miles from this high viewpoint, I thought.

Behind, whence I had come, were the moors with their craggy outcrops; to the east Trencrom Hill and the Godolphin estates, and beyond that Bodmin. To the west was Penzance and my hated Aunt Purity (now I recalled her name). But directly to the south was a wondrous sight.

St Michael's Mount rose from the sparkling sea like something from a fairy tale. A small but towering island, topped by a grand castle, it stood proud and solitary in the wide bay and was separated from the mainland by a short but crucial stretch of sea. All around it, as far as the eye could see, the coast swept in a great protective arm, from the Lizard Point in the far south to Penlee Head in the west. It looked as if the giant who was rumoured to have made his home in the castle on the Mount had one day bent down and, having taken a liking to the look of the land hereabout, had taken an enormous bite out of the county and swallowed it whole.

The Mount. The idea of it made the hairs prickle on the back of my neck. Mam had always said it was a magic place, served by a secret, hidden road which lay beneath the sea. I imagined the giant who lived there, the one who had skipped stones across the sea to make the Scilly Islands; the one who plucked sailors from their boats to eat for dessert, whose breath made the fog that rolled in over the land at dawn. And not only the giant lived there. It was a place frequented by pirates and mermaids and all manner of other exciting beings. It was hard to tear my eyes away from it.

The kitten howled, its eyes narrowed at me.

"Have at you!" I cried and adopted an exaggerated swordman's stance, one hand curled over my head, the other wielding an invisible blade. I danced about the hillside, fighting – as my imagination would have it – a black-bearded Barbary pirate in the company of the fire-haired warrior chief. The pirate I fought was one of those

45

who had raided Penzance, which Da had told me about, for it had happened in his time. Pirates had come from far away, he said, from Northern Africa with swords as curved as sickle moons, all the way to Cornwall to steal people away to sell as slaves. They had sailed right into Mount's Bay — three big, square-sailed caravelles stuffed with Barbary raiders — and no one had stopped them. And there they had attacked a church full of folk at Sunday worship one summer morning, and made off with sixty of our countryfolk, most of whom were never seen again. So caught up in my imaginings was I that when a voice said, "Ho, boy! Have you killed him yet, your opponent?" I almost leapt out of my skin.

A little old man stood there, puffing from the climb, and leaning on his stick for support. "Don't know what you mean, sir," I said, very much taken aback. I felt his eyes boring into me.

"Mock battle, is it?" he said, amused. "A Spaniard, perhaps, with a burnished breastplate and oiled moustaches? Or maybe a pirate with a hook for a hand and a cutlass as curved as a sickle moon?"

I couldn't stop staring at him: his regard was so odd. His eyes were black, mesmerizing. Or at least one was black; the other was an honest brown. My gaze slid back to the black eye, which gleamed at me brighter than any Spaniard's armour. "Do you read minds, sir?" I asked, awed.

The old gentleman laughed. "Not I. My cat, though, has a remarkable aptitude in such matters."

And suddenly there had appeared at his feet a very smart-looking mackerel-striped tabby cat, which gazed at me with bright yellow eyes. At the sight of this larger, well-set-up animal, my own kitten came bounding back across the turf and fair hurled itself at my ankles.

"Your cat reads minds?" I asked, intrigued.

"My cat knows many things. He is far-travelled and as wise as an owl. I see you have a fine feline companion as well." The kitten was now looking up at the man with its ears laid back. "What is his name?"

He could not have asked me a more difficult question, for in truth the chet had no name, at least none I had given it. I shrugged, still unable to stop staring at his odd eyes.

"What, you don't know the name of your cat? Then I see you must be independent travellers, for if you do not know the name of a thing, you cannot own it!"

He smiled more widely and I saw now that he had a gold tooth. This, too, caught my fascination.

"And what is your name, lad? No – don't tell me, let me guess." He closed his eyes for a moment and I felt a sort of relief, as if I had been rooted to the spot and was now free to move once more. My kitten mewed and was answered by the tabby cat, and the next thing I knew, the old man said, "I see . . . a J." His eyelids flicked open as sharply as if they had been on springs, making me jump.

"That, that'll be Jude, sir," I said, flustered.

"Ah, Jude, is it?" He took a step forward and grasped me

by the shoulder, a movement so spritely that it took me quite by surprise, as did the power of his grip, which seemed not at all like that of an old man. Closer up, I could see that he was not lined as much as I would have expected in one so grey-haired, and his black eye did not move as the brown eye did but sat there in the socket as still as a stone, but as shiny as water.

He winked, then made a complicated gesture. The eye fell out into his free hand and I yelped in horror. He tossed it into the darkening sky, and the setting sun sent streaks of red light scintillating off it, so it was as if he had plucked it out by the root, leaving it all bloody. All this time, his grip on my shoulder remained unwavering, and I had the sudden awful thought that perhaps he was the Devil, especially since Mam said that he often appeared to folk at twilight, which was neither day nor night.

"Lost the original at sea, boy," he said, popping the terrible orb back in again. "Little scrap with a Dutch privateer, you know how it is." I did not, but I said nothing. "Now then, Jude – which is an ill-omened name if ever there was one – you may call me Uncle Momo. Where are you off to at this chancy time of the day? What would such a fine, if ragged, lad be doing out on his own when all other young lads are making their way home for their supper?" The brown eye blinked, but the horrid black eye kept staring right at me as if it could see into my very soul. The mackerel cat was staring at me too, its yellow eyes pale and glittery.

48

"Perhaps," Uncle Momo went on, "perhaps, I say to myself, the lad is out on an adventure. Perhaps the lad *has* no home. . ."

He looked at me expectantly, and I stared back at him aghast. Mam had her moments of knowing others' thoughts, but she made no attempt to terrify them with that knowledge.

"I must be on my way." I tried to pull my arm away from those steely fingers. "My mam will be wondering where I've got to."

"Oh, I don't think she will. Even a poor woman would not allow her son to go about in a smock in such need of a wash, nor with his hair as shaggy as a moorland pony's. So I am thinking to myself, perhaps the lad is in need of a feed. Perhaps he and his kitten should come with me and Amoush here to the Mount of St Michael the Avenging Angel, where the good Mary will give them each something to eat and a bed for the night."

"The Mount?" What serendipity was this? "You live on the Mount?"

Seeing that he had caught my interest, the old man winked. "I am one of that privileged few, yes indeed. Whenever I return to these shores, that is the place I call my home."

"I have heard many . . . strange things about the Mount."

"Ah, well that will be because it's a passing strange place."

"And a hard place to get to?"

He cocked his head at me. "Without a boat 'tis a devilish job."

"Do you go by boat?"

"Sometimes I do; and sometimes I don't."

"So you know about the secret path, then?" I breathed, all fear of him forgotten.

He leaned towards me, tapped the side of his nose. "It has revealed itself to me, on occasion."

I was thinking fast now, and proud of myself for that fact. In the heat of all that thought it seemed very likely to me that if I could get to the Mount then no one would be able to take me away from there, not to the workhouse, nor to my detested aunt. But some caution had also crept into these thoughts, reminding me it was possibly not sensible to go with a strange man to an island from which no one could rescue me. Craftily, I asked, "Will you show me the secret road?" Because then, I thought, I can go with him and return if I do not like the place.

He put an arm around my shoulder. "Your mam is dead, is she not?" he said with such a blaze of sympathy in his expression that I felt the tears spring to my eyes.

"Aye, sir. And my da too."

And I blurted out how Mam had been a wise woman, and how even so the plague had taken her, and how I missed her; and how Da and I had fended for ourselves, until. . . I could not get the words out.

His mackerel cat came and stood before me then,

regarding me with its hard yellow eyes, its gaze so piercing that I suddenly felt quite ill.

"Ah, down a great deep hole, was it?" the old man said as if to himself. "That'll be one of the mines, then, I reckon? I'd heard about that this morning in the market."

I gulped back my rising sobs. "There was an accident, and my da. . ."

He shook his head. "Ah, a rum do, that. They say a charge went off too early, brought a fall down on the man inside."

I nodded dumbly, my throat stoppered.

"Poor powder claims lives. I've known a few boys lost that way in my time. So that was how your da went, was it?"

The tears sprang out, despite all my efforts to hold them back. But instead of regarding me with disgust, the old man watched me kindly.

"It's no disgrace to weep for your da, nor your mam neither. 'Tis no easy thing to be an orphan. Am I right in that, eh, lad? That there's no one left to care for you?"

"Th-there's an aunt in Penzance. . ."

His eyes narrowed. "And your aunt, does she know you were on your way to her?"

"Oh, I wasn't! I don't like her and I'm sure she don't like me. She's called Purity, you see, and she's a . . . a Bible-basher!" This made him chuckle, and my heart warmed to him. "But if it's not to her I go then they say I'm for the workhouse in Bodmin."

"Bodmin, is it?" Uncle Momo clicked his tongue. "You don't want to go there."

I shook my head, entirely in agreement.

"So if you come with me and Amoush, then no one will miss you and start a hue and cry?"

I shook my head again.

"So here you are, a penniless orphan all alone in the world, with just your nameless little cat for company, eh? Well, it seems to me that a charitable man should take you both under his wing and offer you both a square meal. We'll make our way over to the Mount and my good Mary will serve you up a slice of hot mutton pie and a pot of creamy milk for your kitten."

"Actually, sir, he prefers cheese to milk," I said truthfully; but my mouth was already watering.

He clapped a hand on my shoulder. "Ah, then cheese it is. Mutton pie for the orphan lad and a chunk of the best yellow cow's cheese for his cat."

At this, the chet mewed plaintively and my stomach rumbled as loudly as cartwheels trundling over cobbles. Looking back now, I might say it was my boyish greed that was my downfall. Once I had thought about that slice of pie steaming away into the rafters of a homely cottage kitchen, with a fire burning merrily in the grate and my chet happily chasing its lump of cheese into a corner, I could think of nothing else. So I followed the old man and his mackerel tabby unsuspectingly down the winding lane towards St Michael's Mount.

8

THE MOUNT

The light had almost fled the sky by the time we came down out of Gulval and crossed the marshes towards the little town of Market-Jew, which lay opposite the Mount. Stars had even started to pop into view, for the sky was cloudless and clear. Soon there were too many of them to count – you might as well try to count the speckles on a starling's wing – and a chill was in the air that made my skin prick with gooseflesh. Seeing the expanse of dark sea where the island rose like a mountain against the greying sky did not help, for it seemed miles away and impossible to reach, secret path or no secret path. I shivered.

"Art cold?" Uncle Momo asked. "I should have thought. Well, we'll be home before too long if the tide is right." He reached out and took my bag from off my back and slung it over his own shoulder. "That will lighten the load," he said and strode away from me before I could say a word of protest, taking bigger, faster strides than I would ever have thought possible in such a greybeard. I had to fair run to keep up with him.

No one moved on the streets of Market-Jew. I had only ever been here once, with Mam on market day. We had hitched a lift in Farmer Scoble's cabbage cart, on top of the turnips and cauliflowers, the spuds and kale. We didn't sit on the eggs, though: they were nestled in two big baskets of straw up at the front, and Mam said they were worth more than all the rest put together because of the gold they held within. It was only when Farmer Scoble dropped one getting the basket down and it cracked on the cobbles, bleeding its yolk out in a glistening golden puddle, that I understood what she meant. On market day the town had been bustling, crammed with people and animals and noise. Sheep and cattle and geese had filled the livestock market; chickens squawked and dogs had run about barking. Girls eyed up the local boys and children milled around the taffy-man, hoping for a free treat. Now it looked a very different sort of place, shadowy and sinister, like an abandoned village, somewhere not quite real.

The mackerel tabby which the old man had called Amoush now ran out in front of us with its tail held high in the air. It miaowed loudly, and my kitten popped its head out of my pocket and mewed back.

The old man smiled. "Well, now," he said. "Byasen. That's a funny name for a cat. What's it mean?"

I stared at him, very confused by this. First of all, I didn't know whose name Byasen could be. And secondly, every Cornishman knows that the word means "pied bird" or magpie. That was when realization struck me with a chill that felt like ice in my belly. Byasen. It was the name of my chet, my little pied kitten; and I had not known it, but somehow the information had been transferred between my kitten, the mackerel tabby and the old man.

Now heat followed cold. Black stars danced before my eyes. I thought he had been teasing when he told me his cat read minds.

"Byasen," I echoed stupidly. "It means magpie. In Cornish."

Uncle Momo looked cross. "Of course it does," he said shortly, as if angry with himself for forgetting such a thing; but something in me knew. He was not from here. He was a stranger. That should have sealed my suspicions and made me turn back, but I did not. Fate seemed to have me in its grip. Who can say how momentous decisions in your life are ever made? Had I turned on my heel and sought out the sharp nose and bitter tongue of Aunt Purity, my life would have gone in a very different direction to the one it took, and maybe I would not be here telling you this strange tale.

Byasen now ducked his head back down into my pocket and turned around a couple of times in there as if preparing himself to go to sleep. When I thought of how he and Amoush had spoken together up on Castle an Dinas hill I felt all at once even more alone. Had it told the old man's cat the first letter of my name? If so, how should a chet know such a very human thing? Had it told the tabby I was homeless, without anyone to look out for me? I had thought it was my friend: now I began to wonder whether cats were to be trusted at all.

As if I had no control over my feet, I trudged after the old man striding towards the foreshore with the cat at his heels.

Down there, the sea was all black and silver, little rills of surf rolling softly against the shingle. The surface of it gleamed and glittered. It looked like a great dark serpent, coiling and uncoiling, and hissing all the time. I hesitated in fear, but the old man did not pause. Instead he walked right up the edge of it and the mackerel cat followed, raising its paws high and fastidious, stepping elegantly from stone to stone. Did he mean to walk right into the sea? But then I came up alongside him and saw, like a ghost, a stone causeway all pale and silvery-gold, just below the lapping waves; and with each moment that we stood there regarding it, the causeway grew closer and closer to the surface until at last the first stones were revealed, broaching the water like a fish's back, shiny and slick in the moon's light.

The old man bent down, picked up Amoush and set it on his shoulder, on top of my sack, and there it wove itself about his neck, for all the world like a living neckscarf. Then he tapped his stick on the causeway and said, "Here's your secret path then, Jude. Are you ready to take it?"

I took a deep breath, as if to cry out "No!" but then he added quickly, "I can almost smell Mary's mutton pie from here," and my stomach growled inside me like a trapped lion cub.

Even so, as he set his foot upon the secret path, tapping

with his stick for the best footing, I lagged behind. But what choice did I have? Everything I owned in the world was on the old man's back. Besides, there was that mutton pie. . . Oh, how I concentrated on the bright egg glaze decorating its pastry cap, which glowed in the candlelight like molten gold; on the juicy meat and luscious gravy that lurked within! By the time we were halfway across the causeway my mouth was so full of water of my own making that I was fit to drown in it without ever touching the sea.

The chet had levered itself upright in my pocket, its two front paws with their little white socks poking over the edge of the fabric. Seeing itself to be in the middle of the ocean, it let out the most piteous wail. The mackerel cat draped around its master's shoulders lifted its head and gave a long, low growl, and after that the kitten dropped back into the pocket and did not stir again, though I felt its breath come fast and shallow through the thin cloth of my smock, as if it were full of fear but dared not show it.

On we went, and by now the stones were high and drying in the night air, for the tide was going out and our path stretched clear before us all the way to the island. I had been watching my feet till now, so that when I looked up I was taken aback by how the Mount reared up before me, dark and brooding. At the foot of the hill on which sat the castle, an entire village lay nestled, with lights at the windows and boats bobbing at anchor behind the protective arms of a harbour wall. My heart lifted. The magic of the place had drawn me but in truth I had feared what might be revealed when we got there – the pirates and mermaids seemed less exciting – and more downright terrifying – as the prospect of actually encountering them drew near. I was relieved to see no patch-eyed, stubble-jawed men sharpening their cutlasses; nor sharp-toothed, fish-tailed maidens surveying the waters for a likely sailor to drown. Instead, it looked quite ordinary and familiar: a proper little Cornish fishing village inhabited by ordinary Cornish fishing folk.

Except . . . the old man who led me across the shining secret path was no man of Kernow, for he had not known the Cornish name for magpie. The thought kept nagging at me and would not leave me alone.

It was not unheard of that outlanders came to live in our remote corner of the world, but it was rare. Darker-skinned men were seen from time to time at the docks at St Ives or Penzance, but mostly they were just more weathered than other folk, or they had shipped in with an exotic cargo and would ship out again with some Cornish tin or wool. They did not stay. Few lived here, like Old John's friend, Abdellah. I had heard there was a woman of Spain who lived in Mousehole, the sole survivor of a vessel that went down in a storm off Tater Du, the Black Rock. And there were wandering folk in ragged clothes and wearing baubles in their ears who told fortunes and sold strange wares, whose children tumbled acrobatically and juggled coloured balls. They called themselves 'Jiptians: others called them gypsies and were glad to see the back of them, claiming them to be dangerous and foreign, as if the two things went hand in hand. And although I did not think the old man was an Egyptian, his skin was a shade or two darker than most. And he did not know the Cornish word for magpie. . .

All this occupied my thoughts as the island came closer and closer, until suddenly there was the crunch of shingle as the old man set foot on solid ground. I turned and looked back and there was the causeway, its seawashed stones smooth and gleaming, all the way back to Market-Jew, and as straight as an arrow, as if fairy folk had laboured out of sight beneath the waves to bring it into being.

"There now, Jude, you've done what not many can claim to have done: crossed the sea without wood between you and the waves!" Uncle Momo threw back his head and laughed and laughed, and his mackerel cat unwound itself from around his neck and leapt sinuously down to the ground, not making the slightest sound as it landed.

9

"GOODWIFE" MARY

We wove up the hillside along a lane where the cottages lay tumbled together like kittens sleeping in a pile. Above us rose the structure of the great castle itself, easily big enough for a giant to inhabit. *Grind his bones to make my bread* was the phrase that played itself over and over in my head. For a brief moment of ecstasy and terror I thought Uncle Momo would take me there and give me over to the giant, and had been out walking the countryside with the express purpose of finding lost boys to feed to him. But just before we reached the gates the mackerel cat shot off to the right and vanished into the darkness. Uncle Momo followed.

Fear now began to grip me as we left the lights of the little settlement behind us. All I could see as we rounded the point was the sea stretching silver and uncaring to the far horizon; that and the towering black rocks above and down below, far below, the low murmur and suppressed roar of the sea. All at once I was overcome by a sensation as if someone had picked me up and spun me around and then placed me back on the ground again so that my knees and head felt as wobbly as frogspawn.

"Wait!" I called out. "Wait, I am dizzy!"

He turned, and the moon struck his face so that the black eye was like the sea, full of silver light, flat and gleaming and inhuman. Now I really did regret my decision to follow him here. Who was he, really? What sort of a name was Uncle Momo? And why did he not know the Cornish word for magpie?

"Fear not, young Jude," Uncle Momo said. "You're dizzy because of the lack of food in your belly. But Mary will soon take care of that." And he reached out and took me by the arm as if to support me.

His fingers were like iron, far stronger than an old man's should be. With them, he propelled me onwards, as if he had read the distrust in my eyes.

"Do you live in this wild place then?" I asked. "Away from the village?" I trotted beside him, staring into the darkness and trying hard not to think of the sheer drop below.

He gave a short bark of a laugh. "From time to time, when I am not on my travels."

"And where do you travel to, sir?" I asked, keen to distract myself from all my misgivings. But if I had been hoping that his answer might reassure me, I was sorely wrong.

"Ah, here and there, lad. Wherever there's gold to be had."

Gold.

A chill ran through me. "Gold is a curse," I heard Mam saying, "and a temptation, even to the best of men." I did not think the greybeard was the best of men, and the presence of the coins in my sack made me even more nervous.

I stumbled along that dark path with a pied cat in my pocket, my arm gripped by a nameless stranger, following the snaky, patterned back of the mackerel cat, into my unknown future, knowing myself an empty-head, and a trusting fool.

At last we came to a halt, and ahead of us something glowed in the darkness. I saw that a cottage had been built into the rocky cliff and that a candle burned in one window, its light blurry and unclear, as if seen through fog. Uncle Momo caught me staring.

"No glass here, lad. When a south-westerly blows in nothing but skin'll withstand it."

"Skin?" Prickles ran up and down my spine.

But he was not listening to me. Instead he took an immense black key from his pocket and applied it to an invisible door to the left of the skin-window. Why would he need a key? Was his "good wife" Mary not within, baking a mutton pie? Someone must be in there. Nobody wasted a good tallow candle by leaving it burning all day in an empty house. The home that I had left that morning had neither lock nor key. "What need?" Mam had laughed. "We have nothing to steal. Besides, if you must lock folk out of your home, what hope is there for the world?"

But as the old man ushered me inside, I realized with a

sudden chill in the pit of my stomach that the key was not required to keep folk out . . . but to keep them in.

I will never forget my first sight of that place: it will be etched in my memory till my dying day, for the moment I entered that house was the moment my life changed for ever.

Inside the cottage a dozen pairs of eyes surveyed me. Most of them were in shadow so that I could not make out their owners. But one presence in particular seized my attention: a gigantic figure with skin the colour of an uncased conker, its head wrapped in a coloured cloth and with a golden earring dangling from one ear, who grinned at me with teeth that shone as white as snow. It wore an apron of sacking such as Mam sometimes wore for cleaning the hearth, and wielded a wooden spoon with which it had been tending an evil-smelling stew which bubbled and frothed on an old iron range.

"Ho there, Mary!" the old man now addressed this person, "I've brought another mouth for you to feed."

Mary? *Mary?* I stared at the odd figure in consternation, for despite the name and the clothing it was surely no woman, and certainly not the "good wife" Uncle Momo had mentioned. Rather it seemed to be a dark-skinned giant of a man with bright black eyes and the traces of a beard. The hand which clutched the wooden spoon was vast and knuckly; and the forearm to which it was attached was sinewy and criss-crossed with pale scars.

Seeing my puzzlement, the old man laughed. "His real name is Mahmoud el Fezani; but I find Mary less of a mouthful."

The dark man gave a lopsided grin and replied in a harsh-sounding, heathenish tongue, to which the greybeard replied in the same language.

I gazed into the shadows as my eyes became accustomed to the gloom and found there four or five boys rather older than I, two girls with hair as pale and fine as thistledown; and an older lad with a wide gap between his front teeth and a prominent forehead which made it look as if he were growing horns.

"Who are these people?" I asked then. "Are they your children, sir?"

Uncle Momo chuckled. "Well, bless the boy," he said. "For a man with no wife other than Mary here, that would be fine work indeed!" He walked into the shadows and there clutched against him one of the girls, who looked so frail and dainty I fear she might snap in two at his touch, and the boy next to her, a strapping lad who might well pull a plough if the horse fell sick. "Do you see the family resemblance, Jude? No?" And he threw back his head and let a great bellow of a laugh roar up into the rafters.

"No, sir," I replied in a low voice. "But if they are not your relatives then I am left wondering who they are."

"No need to concern yourself with such fine distinctions, Jude. Here we are all one big, happy family.

64

Aren't we, Jack?" His black eye roved over them and the candlelight reflected in it in the most demonic way.

The boys nodded silently. One murmured, "Aye, sir," as if on board a ship, and the gap-toothed boy just grinned vacantly.

If this was meant to reassure me it was not working. "I beg pardon, sir, but I think I had best be going to my aunt in Penzance. My neighbours, the Scobles, will have told her I'm on my way: they are farming folk and . . ." I was babbling now ". . . and most conscientious in their duties and they said they were going to tell her. They'll all be wondering where I am. I'm sure they'll come looking for me." As I lied, I inched towards the door. I had no plan in my mind other than to run as far and as fast from here as I could and lie in wait down at the little shingle cove for the secret path to reveal itself once more so that I could scarper across it back to the mainland, never to set foot on this accursed island ever again.

Uncle Momo beamed at me. "You're here now, lad, and here you'll stay. Mary'll give you a ladle of stew, won't you, Mary?"

At this, the dark man waved his spoon at me. My stomach felt as empty as a sea cave, but I shook my head resolutely. "No, thank you, sir, I won't trouble you further." I reached behind me and laid a hand on the doorknob and turned it as quietly as I could; then quick as a flash I turned and pushed it with all my might.

I had expected to be catapulted out into the darkness,

on to the narrow, stony path high above the sea; but the door did not budge an inch. With a sinking heart I remembered the great iron key. When I turned back, shaking, Uncle Momo waved this object at me. He clucked his tongue and said regretfully, "It seems the lad is not as grateful for our hospitality as he should be, Mary. But then, he has not tasted your fine stew yet, and that will surely make all the difference."

He came bounding forward out of the shadows then and laid hold of me and I yelled and yelled. Byasen mewed and howled, crushed up against my chest. "Let me go!" I got away from him for a moment, enough to kick at the door and make its hinges rattle; but still it would not open and all the children laughed at my pathetic efforts to save myself.

Now he ushered me to the table and pushed me down on to the settle and a bowl of stew was placed before me. It was grey and thin-looking, even less appetizing than the meals Da and I had scraped together for ourselves; and it tasted worse than anything I have eaten from that day to this. But it is remarkable what a hungry boy will eat when the pangs are upon him, so I bent my head and shovelled the contents of the bowl into my mouth with the hunk of stale bread they gave me and before long the bowl was empty except for a few bones, some gristle and what looked suspiciously like lumps of matted fur, as if a few desperate mice had drowned themselves in the pot. Byasen craned his neck over the top of my pocket, his nose sniffing and twitching, and then without a by-your-leave he leapt down on to the table, stuck his head in the bowl and swallowed the lumps of fur and gristle whole, then applied himself to the bones, chasing them round and round the bowl with his face till they jumped out on to the table, where he set the side of his mouth to them and cracked them with alacrity.

Uncle Momo clapped his hands. "Right then, young 'uns: show's over and it's time for you to turn in."

I yawned hugely. My head spun – from fear and exhaustion, or from whatever was in the stew? The next thing I knew I was dozing with my head on my hands at the table. I blinked and hazarded a glance around. Momo and "Mary" were sitting by the fire talking in low voices. The mackerel cat lay curled comfortably between them, the firelight gleaming redly on its striped furry back.

"He very young," Mary said, and I remember being surprised that he spoke English, albeit with a strange accent.

"Not too young, I think."

"Maybe not, but is he strong?"

"He's of local peasant stock. They breed them sturdy in this place."

Mary nodded. "He has unusual look. Those eyes, such a piercing blue. That may help. Or we keep him here a year or two, feed him up till he fills out. He fetch more then."

Uncle Momo shook his head. "I need the money now, not in a year or two. Who knows where any of us will be by then?"

I kept my head pressed against the hard wood of the table and sucked my breath in to keep myself from screaming out. Being kept in this place for two days, let alone two *years*, was unimaginable. And what was all this talk about filling me out so that I fetched more money? As for where we would all be in two years, Uncle Momo and the strange dark man called Mary would be dancing at the end of a rope if I had my way. My heart beat loud and fast and I vowed that I would escape this place by hook or by crook as soon as ever I could.

As if it had read my mind, the mackerel cat raised its head and looked straight at me. Then it miaowed loudly. "Is he, now?" Uncle Momo said, frowning. He got to his feet. "Well, we can't have that."

He came over to the table and shook me roughly by the shoulder. "Eavesdropping, were you, lad? Your ma should have taught you that eavedroppers rarely hear good of themselves."

Actually, Mam had always told to keep my ears open and listen carefully to what folk said, for you never knew what useful information you might come by, but I did not say anything, and instead yawned hugely and feigned sleepiness, groaning and rubbing at my eyes as if he had woken me out of a deep slumber.

"Off to bed with you," the old man said, propelling me to my feet and pushing me in front of him to the door in the shadows. This, he opened. It was dark in there and filled with the sound of snoring and the whuffling of many people breathing at once. The slice of light which fell from the outer room into the inner revealed a tumble of bodies lined up on the floor head to tail like pilchards pressed into a barrel. Then there came a hard push in my back and I stumbled and sprawled amongst them.

Curses flew; fists and feet too. "Get off, you clumsy oaf!" was the least of it.

Grudgingly, they made a narrow space for me and I lay down, as stiff and straight as a stick. "Why are you all here?" I asked into the darkness after a while. "What do they mean to do with me?"

For a long time no one replied. Someone laughed, a high-pitched snicker of derision at my idiocy. Then a girl's voice said, "Jude is it? You are well named, for you are among the unluckiest people in the world."

HARD LABOUR

All that night I hardly slept, but tossed and turned, wondering why I had been brought to this place. Time and again my mind circled back to the idea that Uncle Momo supplied local butchers with a very particular sort of tender, fresh and plump cut of meat; and that the skin which covered the window where the candle burned had once belonged to a boy much like myself. By the time dawn finally came I had convinced myself that the next day would be my last.

As the light crept in, I saw that there were above a dozen of us in crammed into that room, of all sizes and types, and aged from ten or so years of age to those approaching their majority. As I sat up and stared at them all, wondering how they had come to be here and for what reason, the boy with the bulging forehead sat up and fixed me with his fish-like eyes.

"Where you from?"

"Kenidjack Vale," I mumbled.

"Never heard of it." He stared at me suspiciously. "How did he come to take you? Where's your ma and pa?"

I said nothing, willing him to shut up.

"Been taken to the county gaol, have they? You've the look of a bad 'un, I'd say."

I could feel tears gathering behind my gritty eyes. "They're dead," I said quietly. I felt my fists balling.

The fish-eyed boy grinned. "Spoiling for a fight, are you?" He jabbed me in the chest, and I felt a red tide begin to rise in me. I was about to take a swing at him when one of the thistle-headed girls stepped between us.

"Don't pay any attention to Jack Two," she said. "His da was hung from the Trethevy gibbet."

"Hanged," corrected her sister. "Honestly, Alice, 'tis shameful you forget your lessons so fast. It's pheasants that are hung, and men that are hanged."

"Grammar be damned: they both end up swinging from the neck!" boomed a deep voice on the other side of the door. There came the rattle of a key in a lock and the creak of hinges and suddenly there was Uncle Momo in the doorway, the mackerel cat at his heel. I wondered what had become of Byasen. "Now, now, Jude, no greeting for your Uncle Momo?" He put an avuncular arm around me and propelled me out into the main room. "And what a surprise you've turned out to be! 'Tis like having royalty to stay, is it not, Mary?"

Mary was standing at the range, stirring the iron cookpot with a ladle so large it made the muscles stand out hard on his vast, meaty arms. I felt my stomach lurch up into my mouth. What was in that pot, and what would soon join it?

"It is, Momo," he grinned. "He a rare find indeed." And he spooned some of the contents of the cookpot into a bowl and passed it to the old man.

I could feel the curious eyes of my fellow captives upon me as Uncle Momo sat me down at the bench and set the bowl of steaming stuff before me.

But out of the huge pot came not boiled flesh and bones but a greyish porridge which appeared to have nothing more sinister in it than oats and water. I surprised myself by eating hungrily.

"That's right: eat up, my boy. We must take care of the gifts that God grants us. Who could have known that such a ragged lad should be so blessed?"

He had found my gold. A dull, heavy sensation pervaded my stomach. Then something touched my leg, making me jump, and I glanced down to find the chet there, tapping me with a paw. His eyes were huge: he jumped up into my lap.

Uncle Momo sat down beside me. "Now, then, Jude: best tell me the truth about your parentage: who are your family and where do they live?"

"I have told you true, sir: my da died in the mine and my mam of the plague."

"Then whence come these? Did you rob them?" He took my sack and upended it and out rolled the contents. Momo pushed my clothes and threw the lodestone into a corner of the room as if it were a piece of rubbish, until just the bright golden coins remained.

"Come along, Jude," Momo said softly. "You're among friends here. Tell me where you got the gold."

And so I told him where we had got the gold from and how Mam said it was a curse and buried it in the garden, beneath the beehives, and all the while Uncle Momo watched me with his dead black eye. "So, there's no rich family behind thee, then, lad?"

I shook my head.

"That's a shame," he said quietly. "For if there had been you might be going back to them."

It seemed I had made a misstep by telling the truth. "My Aunt Purity, who is my da's sister, has some money," I said quickly. "I'm sure she does: she lives in a nice house in Penzance town."

But Momo shook his head. "Rich men don't toil down mines. It seems you must stay with us for now, young Jack." And he scooped up the coins and stashed them away inside his coat.

"Jack? My name's Jude, not Jack!"

"Ah, now that's where you're wrong, lad. There are no Judes here. We have only Jacks and Jills; and since you'll be staying with us Jack you'll be from now on: Jack. . ." He calculated slowly, ticking off the fingers of each hand, and at last pronounced, "Jack Seven. Aye. Jack Seven it is."

Jack Seven. I shivered. I had lost my name, and my freedom, and Jack Seven stood for all that. Thus began a new, darker chapter in my poor life.

*

After all had eaten, Uncle Momo took himself off, leaving us with Mary, who took up a length of rope and started to tie us together, each to the next boy by ankle or wrist, with a length of slack between us so we might to some degree move independently. When he passed the cord around my own wrist, I stared at it in disbelief. Tied up with a scratchy old rope, like a donkey being led to market! I tried to snatch my hand away, but Mary's grip was like iron, although he smiled and smiled. "Don't struggle, boy: it go easier for you if you accept the fate that Allah, the All Merciful, send you."

I gazed at him curiously. "Allah? Is that another name for Uncle Momo?" I asked, doubtfully, for the old man seemed to me quite the opposite of merciful.

Mary sucked in his breath and began to mutter furiously in the strange language I had heard him conversing in the night before. At last he said, "Such ignorant infidel. I see we have to pay special attention to you."

Special attention I did not want. I looked away, in sudden panic. Special attention: was that his code for the evening cookpot? Would they fill it with water and repulsive-smelling plants, like Mam did when cooking up a spell? Would they strip me naked and plunge me into it and slowly cook the meat off my bones?

But no: Mary led us out of the house towards the sea, where the remains of an ancient building lay ruined, its roof caved in, its wall tumbled down, and weeds growing amongst its stones in riotous abandon.

"Momo thinking of expanding business." He gestured towards the first heap of rubble. "You clear all this and pile timber and stones outside."

For three days we laboured, under the watchful eyes of Mary and the mackerel tabby. Byasen seemed to have cut his losses. Cats are well known for keeping a weather-eye out for their own comfort, and it seemed to me that the chet had come to the conclusion that his future well-being no longer lay with his old friend but with Uncle Momo's familiar, Amoush. The two of them sat up on the rocks, lazing in the sun, blinking their inscrutable eyes, and it was as if they were laughing at us poor fools.

And so I looked away from them, out at the shining sea and the hazy green-and-gold land beyond and wondered how it had come to this: that I should be a prisoner within sight of the hills where I had wandered happy and free, while Da worked and Mam tended the bees and collected herbs, and I took all for granted and thought such times would last for ever.

11

AN ACCIDENT

Little by little my muscles grew used to the work and my night terrors were numbed. One day I found myself asking the boy next to me, Jack Four, "How did Uncle Momo catch you?"

It was a long yarn he spun me, all about fortune-tellers down in Market-Jew and how he'd spent his last copper on a mutton pasty and was bemoaning the fact loudly when a kindly old gentleman had pressed a penny into his palm and sent him to see the gypsy – a veiled being with black-rimmed eyes, gold earrings and a deep voice.

"That sounds like Mary!" I said.

The fair-haired boy – who turned out to be Jack Five – gave me a doleful look. "If you're so devilish clever, how did you come to be taken in by them?" he said crossly, and turned his back on me.

"Yes, you must be really stupid," said someone else, "having all that gold in your sack and still getting caught. You could have gone anywhere, been anyone, with all that money. But instead you're here, a luckless captive like the rest of us."

A captive I was: no more, nor less. I soon discovered that escape was well-nigh impossible. Uncle Momo and Mary had eyes everywhere, or so it seemed; and some of the older boys acted more like their lieutenants than their prisoners. At night we were securely locked in our crowded room with an old metal pail in the corner which smelled worse than the privy. One night as I moved around the floor, feeling the great, smooth flagstones with the palms of my hands, Agnes, the elder of the two sisters, whispered, "What are you doing?"

"He's looking for a way out," whispered Alice.

"There isn't one," Agnes said softly. "I know: we looked, too, when we first came here. The walls are solid. There was a window once, but it's long been bricked up."

I sat back, defeated. "How did they catch you?"

The two girls exchanged glances. "You tell him," Alice whispered, her eyes filling with tears.

Agnes took a deep breath and seemed to gather herself. "Our father died of the plague, just like your mam did. One day he was as right as rain, and then he got to sweating and complaining of pains in his head and under his arms, and these red patches started breaking out all over his skin. The next day they turned black, and his neck and armpits grew horrible great swellings, and Mother started to cry, 'It's the pest, the pest!' She made us stay upstairs, away from him, but we heard everything: the coughing and the vomiting, and Father crying out for God to spare him. And then he couldn't speak at all because his throat was stopped and all we heard was his terrible, thick breathing. And the day after that, he died."

She delivered all this in a most matter-of-fact fashion, as if she were telling me about the weather, but I stared at her, horrified. Had my poor dear Mam suffered the same dreadful torments? "And then what happened?" I asked.

"Without Father, there was no one to win a living for the family, and we were already struggling to make ends meet. So one week not long after he had died Mother brought us into Market-Jew on the Thursday market. She left us with an old lady while she went to do some business, and then she came back with an old man with a glass eye. . ."

Glass eye? *Glass*. . . So that was what it was. And I had thought it was magic. "Your mam sold you, to Uncle Momo?" It seemed an enormity beyond all understanding.

We sat there in silence for a long while. Then I asked, "What does he mean to do with us?"

The elder of the sisters shook her head. "I don't know."

"One thing I've noticed," Agnes said after some minutes. "Every night for the last three nights Uncle Momo has taken the lantern from its hook and gone outside for a long while."

I had noticed this odd behaviour too. I nodded sagely. "What do you think he's doing?"

Alice sniggered behind her hand. "Going for a good sit-down in the privy," she whispered.

"Alice! Whatever would Mother say?"

78

But Alice was laughing outright now. Her amusement was infectious and soon I was snorting away beside her, and eventually her older sister joined in. We rolled around, holding our sides, until the tears ran down our cheeks. It was the first time I had laughed since before Mam had died, and when that thought occurred to me it sobered me at once.

But the next night when Uncle Momo took the lantern from its hook and left the cottage, closing the door carefully behind him, I watched with renewed curiosity. Where *was* he going? While Mary oversaw the washing and drying of the dishes, I crept to the skin window and peered out. It was hard to see anything even when I pressed my eye up against it, but one corner had come loose and this I prised away a little more, just enough that I could peer out of the small gap it made.

At first, I could see nothing at all, the darkness was so complete: not even the moon or the stars, or their reflection on the black waves below. Of Uncle Momo there was no sign at all. But then, just as I was about to give up, a flash of light split the darkness. Then it was gone, just like that. I waited, not breathing, and moments later the light flashed again and in that split second I saw the old man holding the lantern high above his head with one hand, peering intently out to sea. Then with his other hand he flicked a cloth over the lantern and doused the light. Pitch-blackness returned, and stayed. Uncle Momo made no more signals with the lantern, and nothing out there responded. When he turned, I moved quickly away from the window.

The key rattled in the lock, and the old man stepped inside, looking grim. He shook his head at Mary.

The big foreigner spread his hands. "Perhaps tomorrow, *insha'allah*."

"It had better be tomorrow," Uncle Momo said darkly. "Or the tides will be wrong for a fortnight."

The next day it rained, not just the seeping mizzle that we often suffer in Kernow, but a rain that stung the skin, and bounced back off the ground where it struck. The seagulls sat high on the rocks, raising their voices in complaint; and the cats stayed indoors. The granite was slippery underfoot, and in our hands. I was lifting a great long, speckled slab which had once been a lintel over a door with Jack Three when I stumbled, the rope came taut on me, and the slab slipped out of my hands and landed on Jack Three's foot. He flew over backwards, wrenching his leg badly. The yelp he let out made all the seagulls take to flight, and brought Uncle Momo and Mary at a run. By now, Jack Three's face was scarlet with shock and pain and his teeth were drawing blood from his lip as he bit it, trying not to cry. I crawled over to him, consumed by guilt. What had I done?

"Hey there! What's happened here?"

"It's my foot, sir. I think it's broke!" Jack's voice began to quaver.

With some effort, we moved the lintel off Jack Three. One look at his leg was enough to confirm the injury, for his foot lay at an unnatural angle. Uncle Momo's face seemed to fill with dark blood.

I did not see the blow coming, perhaps because I was blinking away the rain; perhaps because his dead black eye had me transfixed; perhaps because no one had raised a fist to me before in all my life – not Mam, for all my laziness, nor Da for my fears, nor even Farmer Scoble, whose patience I had often tried with the holes I had made in his fences and the eggs I had filched from his henhouse. Uncle Momo's iron knuckles struck me full on the side of my head like a mallet and I flew backwards, my feet slipping and sliding on the wet stones. I fell down hard with my whole skull ringing and hot pain blazing through me like a fire through a hayfield.

"You useless whelp! He was one of my best. Eight or nine guineas he would have got me, even ten!" The old man shook me till my teeth rattled. "You wretch: God curse the day I found you!"

He reached into his coat and I became convinced that he had a knife in there and that he was about to unsheathe it and plunge it into me; but then suddenly there was a miaow, and the mackerel cat appeared as if from nowhere and with a single bound leapt on to its owner's shoulder. It mewed into the old man's ear; and all the while the rain pelted down, sleeking its tabby coat into shiny black streaks. What could be so important that it would bring a cat out of the dry into weather like this? A movement in the grass, a flash of black and white, caught my eye and the next thing I knew, Byasen was at my feet, his ears laid flat to his head, his eyes huge and round.

They're coming.

The voice sounded in my head. I looked around, but no one else was close enough to be speaking so quietly to me. I looked down and the chet looked up at me, and I heard the words again, even louder.

They're coming! Had my cat just spoken to me?

"Byasen?"

Mraaaow!

Suddenly the mackerel tabby flew from Uncle Momo's shoulder and launched himself upon my chet, and a terrible battle ensued, until the old man reached down and grabbed his cat and fairly threw it away from Byasen.

I bent and picked up my chet. He seemed so small and fragile: I could feel his heart beating against my palms. All at once my own fear subsided and in that moment I knew that I was his protector, and he was mine. "It will be all right," I assured him. Then I turned to Uncle Momo.

"I'm more trouble to you than I'm worth, I know it," I said, the rain falling down my cheeks like cold tears. "Keep the gold you took from me and let me go. I will tell no one about you or this place."

Uncle Momo's mouth stretched into a grin. In the dull light, with his skin stretched tight across the bones of his face and the dead, dark, empty eye nearest me more of an absence than a presence, he seemed to me like a skull, a symbol of Death itself, grinning away in an everlasting grimace.

"Sorry, my lad, can't be doing that."

"But I give you my word!"

"Where would I be if I were to take the word of every ragged scrap that crossed my path? I'd be swinging from Trethevy gibbet, that's where, and though the view from there be very pretty, I don't fancy it as the last thing I'll see in this life.

"No, I have other plans for thee, as my good Amoush has reminded me."

A shudder ran through me. Was he going to feed me to the pot? Or make good on his threat to slaughter me like a Michaelmas pig and leave my bones on this godforsaken sward to be picked over by carrion birds?

But whatever my fate was to be I was not yet to discover, for Mary cried out, "A sail, Momo! A sail!"

And when I followed his pointing finger I saw a fine square-rigger outlined against a horizon streaked with the orange fires of sunset.

12

BLACK POWDER

There was an air of barely suppressed excitement from our captors. Uncle Momo and Mary marched us back to the cottage and locked us in. I watched through the corner of the window where I had peeled back the skin as the pair of them walked out to the furthest part of the isle and examined the passage of the distant vessel through a long, dark contraption.

"That's a spyglass!" Jack Four said, jamming his head in the scant space next to mine. "It makes things as are far away seem close up and large."

I frowned. "How? Is it magic?"

He shrugged. "Prob'ly. Uncle Momo treats it as a great treasure. Jack One kicked it over one day in error and it earned him a bad beating. It come from a place called Veniz in Itly and it cost a vast fortune, accordin' to Mary. A 'prentice made it, he said."

"What's a 'prentice?" I asked, curious.

He shrugged again. "Don't really know. Someone as works for someone else, I guess."

"And who did he work for?"

"A man called Gally Leo."

I had never heard of Veniz, or Itly, or of anyone called Gally Leo, though it seemed as likely a name as any for a magician. I applied my eye to the gap in the skin again and watched each of our captors in turn hold the contraption up to look through. I could have sworn Uncle Momo put the thing to his glass eye. The idea made me shiver and I wondered just what it was he might see with it in conjunction with the spyglass.

At that moment, Byasen struggled up out of my shirt. He had, it seemed, been asleep, for he had what Mam laughingly used to call "bed hair" when I stumbled to the table of a morning without passing it by a comb. She would flatten it down with gentle hands, saying, "There. Now you look less of a little savage and more like my Jude." Tears sprang to my eyes at the memory as I stroked the kitten's fur down in the same way. *We have no one but each other now, Byasen*, I thought, but did not say aloud.

Aye, that's the truth, Jude Lanyon. We must look out for each other. Again, the voice in my head.

I stared at the chet. "Did you speak?"

Jack Four gave me a puzzled look. "No." He made a face at me, then pointed a finger towards his temple and made little circles with it. "You should be in Bodmin, you should." He slid down from the window seat and went to join the others in seeing what food they might steal from the unattended cupboards.

85

Byasen's eyes sparkled. *Careful*, he said into my mind.

I was desperate to find out whether I was indeed mad, or whether my cat was actually able to speak to me, but at that moment the key turned in the lock and Uncle Momo and Mary came in, talking nineteen to the dozen in some harsh foreign tongue. Byasen faded into the shadows.

"Jack Seven, come with me!"

Mary pushed me ahead of him into the sleeping room. There we found poor Jack Three lying in a sweat, his pallor making his face a ghastly grey-green in the dim light. When he saw me he smiled, but I could see he was putting the bravest of brave faces on his predicament.

I dropped to my knees beside him. "I am so sorry, Jack. It was my fault for dropping the stone, I know."

He caught my hand. "I don't blame you, Jack," he said feebly. "It could have happened to anyone."

Those words would soon come back to haunt me.

Mary threw an old cambric sheet at me. "Tear into strips!" He went back into the main room and I did as I was told. A minute later he returned with a tin pail of water. "Take off his boot."

Jack Three gazed up, horrified. "Don't touch my foot, please."

I did not want to but I had no choice, for if I did not do it then I knew Mary would with his massive, muscled hands, and I did not think he would be gentle. So I set myself to undoing the knotted leather laces on Jack Three's boots while he told me there was no need and it was just a little sprain and that he would be right as rain in the morning. The wet had made the knots obstinate and my fingers felt as large and useless as sausages.

"Out of way!" Mary pushed me aside. In his hand he held a gleaming knife. It had a wicked, curved narrow blade like the thinnest of new moons, and little patterns were etched all over it.

"No!" I cried. I was sure the dark man was about to do one of us harm, but he simply slipped the blade between the laces and the leather and with a flick of the wrist separated the two as easily as if cutting through water. Inside, Jack Three's foot was a horrible sight: purple with bruises, swollen and misshapen. I gasped.

"What?" Jack Three asked, alarmed. "What do you see?"

I gazed at Mary beseechingly. "Don't cut his foot off," I begged, visited by a sudden awful image of the bloated, purple thing bobbing in tomorrow's stew.

Mary ignored me as he manoeuvred the boot away from the bloated foot with surprising skill. "Ankle is, how say? Out of place. Un-located."

"Dislocated?"

"Dislocated. I need you hold him down while I put back together again."

I did not want to lay hands on him. The idea of the poor, ruined ankle come apart from the leg made me feel faint. But Jack Three's agony was all my fault, and if Mary could help him I knew I must make amends for my clumsiness. So

87

while Mary took hold of the protesting boy's leg with one meaty hand and his foot with the other, I lay across Jack's body to keep him as still as I could. There followed a cacophony of sounds the like of which I never wish to hear again in all my days. A wrenching and a grinding of gristle and bone; an agonized animal howl from Jack Three which made my ears hurt and my teeth clench as his body bucked beneath me. Then the howl ceased and he went abruptly limp. I was quite sure he had died, and cried out.

"Stop your noise and give me sheets." Mary's deep voice broke the eerie silence.

"Are you going to wrap him up and bury him?" I whispered.

Mary grunted. "Foolish child. He not dead, he only faint! Now go get me two pieces of kindling, as straight as you can find, and hurry back."

Off I went, mightily relieved to be out of the torture chamber. I searched through the woodpile by the stove and found two straight sticks. By the time I reluctantly returned, Mary had expertly bandaged the foot and ankle at right angles. Now he took the kindling from me and bound them one on either side of the joint. "To hold the leg straight," he said, "or he never stand true, let alone walk." Just as I was thinking I had misjudged him, he added, "And what use to us is a cripple?"

The cries of pain that had issued from the room had quietened everyone. No one spoke at supper, but ate with their eyes fixed on their bowls.

As for Mary and Momo, well, something was up — anyone could see that. They scoffed their food down at speed, then started to gather a collection of items. From the locked cupboard in the corner of the room came three wooden boxes and some heavy leather pouches. Momo opened the first box and started to lay its contents out on the table. One after another a dozen flintlock pistols appeared. He looked each of them over, testing their mechanisms, blowing in their pans, gazing down their muzzles. Then, apparently satisfied, he laid them back in the box again. He did the same with the other two boxes, then added a pair of long-barrelled muskets. Next, he opened one of the pouches and poured a little of what it contained out into his palm. Its scent wafted to me: dusty and musty. Uncle Momo looked up and found my eyes on him.

"Do you know what this is, young Jack?"

I did. I knew it in the pit of my stomach. And I remembered where I had smelled that smell last. "It's gunpowder," I said flatly.

"Aye, lad. The best to be had in the kingdom of good King Charles."

"Which is not very good at all!" said Mary. They both laughed, and hatred rose up in me. For I had remembered the description my father had given of the man from whom he had bought the deathly powder that had blown him up.

An elderly one-eyed veteran. . . It had been Uncle Momo who had sold my poor da the powder that had destroyed him. I felt my stomach churn and bile rise in my throat. But I forced it down and swore to myself that if ever I had the chance I would avenge my father's death on this monster.

Uncle Momo packed the bags of black powder away in a stout canvas sack, then he took the lantern from its hook and went out into the gloom and did not return for the best part of an hour.

When he came back he looked both crafty and pleased, and full of some diabolic energy. He made us all line up, largest to smallest. I found myself standing next to Agnes as he went from one to the next with a little leather-bound notebook and a stub of pencil.

"What's your real name, Jack One?" he asked the first boy in line.

"Elijah, sir."

"Parish?"

"St Hilary."

Momo wrote this down laboriously, followed by the names and professions of Elijah's next of kin, his age, and his skills, which he gave as "baking bread".

"What's going on?" I whispered to Agnes.

"It's as if he's taking stock," she whispered back. "Like our father used to do at the shop at the end of each week, to see what he had sold and what he needed to buy in."

I made a face. "That doesn't make much sense."

It didn't, then.

Jack Four's real name was Will Tonkin and he came from Mousehole; Jack Five was Ollie Penrose from Penzance, and he said he was a fisherman and good at salting pilchards. Jack Six was from Penberth and was also a fisherman. His real name was Harry Pengelly.

He passed on to Agnes and Alice. Agnes gave their family name as Adams, and Momo beamed. "And you're as fine a pair of Eves as I ever laid eyes on. They'll love such a pretty pair where you're going."

When at last Uncle Momo came to me, I had to admit I had no skills to speak of. In a tight voice I told him, "I cannot work the land, for I am an acknowledged lazybones. My da called me a useless lump when I was down his mine. As for fishing, well, I am afeard of water. . ." And I looked him squarely in his living eye.

Was there a challenge in my regard? Certainly, the old man recoiled; but then he forced a laugh. "Shame that you're afraid of water, laddie, for you'll be seeing a lot of it very soon."

But where *was* my kitten? I looked around but there was no sign of him. "Byasen!" I called, but he did not reply. It seemed he chose to converse only when it suited him, and now that I was about to be taken away, he had disappeared. Would I ever see my little cat again?

At last he stashed his little book away and we were all yoked together by Mary as if we were on our way to work, though by now it was pitch-dark outside. Momo gave the boxes to Jacks One, Two and Four to carry, and the muskets to Jacks Five and Six. To me he gave the sack of gunpowder; to the girls rattling bags of what I imagined must be lead shot. Then he primed and loaded his own pistol, and unlocked the door and ushered us out into the night. Mary followed, with Jack Three slung across his back and a pistol in his hand. The injured boy had regained consciousness, but his eyes shone in the bit of moonlight outside the cottage and I feared that if he set his pain-filled gaze upon me I would be cursed from that day forth.

13

THE CAVE

The moon was elusive as we made our way down the steep rocky path to the shore, a raggle-taggle band tied together by rope and fear. No one spoke. The darkness was oppressive.

It was only as we rounded the headland and the boy at the front of the file cried out that I lifted my eyes from the treacherous path down which we went, and saw the ship. It rode at anchor a quarter of a mile to the lee of the island, bobbing on the black waves. The wind whistled between its masts like the wind in a forest. A gentle tinkle, as of distant bells, sounded at intervals: a sort of discordant music that was both unnerving and lovely.

"It must be a polacca," breathed Jack Five, who prided himself on knowing such things. "I never seen one before: 'tis mighty irregular in these waters."

I understood none of this: to me, with my imagination overworking, it looked like a ghost ship, for shreds of night mist were tangled amidst its sails and there was no sign of any crew; but then Uncle Momo signalled with his lantern — once, twice, three times — and there came an answering flash of light from the anchored vessel.

Even then I did not foresee my fate. I was not a stupid lad, but even after my abduction and captivity and the clues that lay about me, I had no idea of the depths to which men might sink in their morals and their actions for the love of gold. So I stared at the tall ship with my mouth open wide enough to catch a bird, let alone a fly.

"Get on there, you lubbers!" cried Uncle Momo, and we slipped and stumbled our way down to the tiny cove. Once there, the old man took the ends of the rope that bound us together and secured them by means of a great iron hasp to a rusty eye set into the rocks. Then he and Mary walked a little distance away, and vanished.

It was as if the night had swallowed them whole, yet I could hear the crunch of their boots on the shingle as they moved around. Then those steps took on a hollow tone and grew more distant. There was a rumbling sound; then they returned, carrying a long wooden rowing boat overhead. This, they set down in the shallows, and Mary made it fast. Then he and Momo freed us from our bonds and began to seat us in the skiff.

I watched Jacks One and Two squeeze into the bows of the tiny vessel. Then Mary deposited poor Jack Three there too, and I saw how it rocked beneath their weight. A great fear seized me. Surely I would fall overboard and be eaten by the restless, hungry sea. Perhaps the slender boat would overturn and we all would perish. I edged away behind

Jacks Five and Six. Uncle Momo did not seem to notice. My heart began to beat faster. One by one my fellow captives were ranged in the rowing boat until the idea occurred to me that if I were to quietly take to my heels I might leap back up the rocky defile down which we'd come and hare all the way to the settlement of houses on the other side of the island, to where the causeway made its miraculous occasional appearance. I was inching further and further away from the rest of the captives when there shone right in front of me a pair of yellow eyes, burning like small fires in the night.

It was the mackerel tabby cat, Amoush.

It stood squarely in my path and opened its mouth wide, and I knew that it was about to let out a piercing howl and summon its master to let him know one of his prisoners was escaping, but at that very moment a black and white shape flew between us and bowled the mackerel cat over. There ensued a bout of hissing that would shame serpents, but amidst this I heard, quite distinctly, the words, *Run, Jude!*

For a second I was so perplexed that I stayed rooted to the spot.

Run now! The voice came again, and then the black and white shape detached itself from the darkness and I realized it was Byasen, and that he had attacked the mackerel cat for me, though he was half its size.

With an ear-splitting cry, Amoush laid his ears flat to his skull, and hurled himself upon my chet. He buried his teeth in the kitten's throat and with a bloodthirsty growl brought his hind paws up, claws extended, to rake Byasen's unprotected belly.

"No!" I cried, all thoughts of escape gone. I tried to separate the combatants, but only received a cruel clawing for my trouble.

At the sound of the conflict, Uncle Momo's head turned and in three strides he was beside me, grasping my ear between his fingers. "Ow!" I wailed; then he twisted it ever more wickedly and my cry rose as high as a girl's in church.

"Get in the boat!" he snapped.

"I will if you save my little cat."

The old man laughed. "You're in no position to bargain with me, you soft-hearted whelp!" But he let go of my ear and kicked his cat away from mine.

Amoush sprang aside, hissing, his eyes no more than luminous slits, his contempt for all mankind clear in every line of his body. Byasen lay on the ground, his tiny belly puffing in and out. It was too dark to see whether or not he was badly injured. I scooped him up, cradling him against me. Then, before the old man changed his mind, I stuffed him down inside my shirt. "So there we are, Byasen," I whispered, "we shall share each other's fate after all."

Everyone was in the boat now, except for me and Uncle Momo, and it sat perilously low in the water. But the old man seemed unperturbed. "In you go, Jude."

"No, wait," said Mary, and my heart leapt up. Was he going to object that the boat was already too full? Even if I were to be left behind with Uncle Momo and his hellish cat it seemed a better prospect to me than setting out on the heaving black sea that seemed to breathe and swell like some monstrous creature.

"The oars," Mary said. "I forgot the oars."

"God's teeth!" Uncle Momo swore. Then he pushed me. "Go fetch them, boy. You'll be swifter than me. Go along there, twenty feet or so there's a cave. The oars are propped up just inside the entrance. Don't tarry, or even think to escape, for there's nowhere to go from there, just a sheer rock wall and then the sea. Fetch the oars and come straight back, or I'll beat you black and blue!"

Off I went, crunching along the strand to the spot where Uncle Momo and Mary had disappeared, and there was the cave, a place where the dark rock showed a darker absence, like a mouth in the cliff. I stepped into it, and it was like walking from autumn into the depths of winter, so cold was it inside. The oars were just where the old man had said they would be, beyond a thick iron chain that was bolted into each side of the cave, as if to keep people out. I was about to lay hands on the oars when my nose began to twitch and my palms began to itch and burn.

The sensation was unmistakable. "Stop it!" I commanded myself. "What use is gold now?" What use was it ever?

My eyes watered, and I sneezed and sneezed again. When I opened my eyes again I found that I had somehow ducked under the chain and gone much deeper into the cave. The darkness pressed all around me like a pair of cold, clammy hands. And more than darkness. Even though the pale moonlight outside could not penetrate the depths of the cave I knew there was gold here: a lot of gold.

It made me shiver all over.

"Jack Seven!"

Uncle Momo's roar thundered through the air, shocking me from the strange reverie into which I had fallen. Forcing myself to turn around, I stumbled back to the mouth of the cave, grabbed up the oars and legged it out of there. I clutched the wooden paddles to me so hard that Byasen, crammed inside my shirt, gave a yelp.

"I am here, sir. It was so dark in there I almost missed them."

Uncle Momo's dead black eye fell upon me and again I had the sense that it could see right through to the core of me. But if it saw my secret I did not know, for Momo said nothing. He snatched the oars from me and marched me to the boat. My wits were still not fully recovered, for, getting into the skiff, I missed my step and went sprawling and the boat rocked wildly. Water splashed over the sides and everyone cried out.

Momo released the rope that tied us to solid land, threw the oars to Mary and leapt aboard – too swift, too agile for a man of his age. Then he picked me up by the scruff of my neck and sat me down between Agnes and Alice. Mary settled the oars in the rowlocks and began to scull away with powerful strokes and we were borne away on the sea.

14

THE SHIP

How we made it across that expanse of water without perishing, I do not know, but I was seized by terror all the way. Never had I experienced such an unnatural movement as to be inside that little boat with the dipping, rolling ocean all around and beneath. Nothing was solid: everything was fluid and chancy in that strange, watery realm beneath the silent stars. No one spoke. The only sound came from the rhythmic dipping of the oars in and out of the water. Almost, I could not believe in it but felt that I was in a dream – or rather, a nightmare from which there was no escape.

A thick black rope ladder hung down from the side of the tall ship that loomed above us.

"Up you go!" Momo growled, and pushed me towards it. I took a step from the boat to the ladder, and both wobbled so badly that I thought I would fall between them into the sea and be lost for ever. Then I had two feet on the ladder, with my face pressed against the rope, smelling the pungent tar in it, my heart thundering. Up I went, hand over hand, with my knees like water, till I pitched over the gunwale, face down on to the deck.

When I looked up, I knew at once that I was in a foreign land. All around me, limned by the silver light of the moon, were not ghosts, but strange men. Dark of skin they were, and black of eye; sharp-nosed and raw-boned. Some wore a length of cloth wrapped about their heads. Some had shaved all the hair from their crowns so that their skulls shone. Some wore silver earrings hanging from their earlobes. At their sides they all bore curving swords in patterned scabbards, and decorated pistols with long, etched barrels. Their faces were narrow, their movements quick and agile, and they spoke to one another in a language I could not understand. Their breeches reached only as far as their knees and they were barefoot, their toes splayed against the wooden deck like claws. I looked from one to another of them and the curious thought struck me that it was as if I were aboard a vessel crewed by a band of giant, intelligent rats. Then my wits reasserted themselves and I knew them to be men; but I wondered whence in the world they had come, for it was from no place I could imagine.

The same sense of dislocation had affected my companions, who started to whisper amongst themselves and to huddle together. Little Alice began to cry. Uncle Momo hove into view, and behind him Mary, half-carrying Jack Three. We were herded into a straggling line, and

Momo fixed poor Alice with his black glass eye. "Stop your weeping," he told her fiercely, "or I'll stop it for ye."

Jack Three was deposited between me and Jack Five. "Keep him upright," Mary said. "If he falls, you'll be sorry. And you," he hissed at the injured lad. "You'd better play your part well or you'll surely regret it."

All pretence of good nature had deserted our two captors now that they were close to their goal, whatever that might be.

We were joined by two of the ship's crew: a tall man with his head wrapped in a great swathe of white cloth so that it looked as if he wore a gigantic onion, and a grim-looking fellow with what Mam would have called "a hatchet-face" who had a long, thin pigtail growing out of the crown of his head. He had no other hair at all. The second man carried a length of beaded string and a cudgel stuck with nails. The contrast between these two items struck me forcibly, the one being so delicate, the other so fearsome. It seemed to me that we children were stranded somewhere between these two objects, as if between two worlds, belonging neither to one nor the other: too old for childish toys, but yet too young and innocent to be taking up such violence as the massive weapon offered. The face of the onion-headed man was half-turned towards me, lit eerily by the silver moon. He seemed like some great predator, a lion or an eagle: his eyes pinned me to the spot as if I were his prey, though they were lazy and slitted, half-shut as though he were not fully awake. He reminded me a little of the big sandy tomcat who was probably Byasen's father, who spent most of his life lazing in the meadow grass apparently half asleep – until some barely perceptible motion would attract his attention and he would suddenly uncoil himself like a tensioned spring, leap up into the air and deliver a stunning blow with all his might to the unsuspecting mouse or vole which had had the misfortune to cross his path. Then he would stretch himself out again with his prize between his paws, and bat it around until at last he would grow bored with the play and toss it into the air, and swallow it head first, fur and all. This man reminded me of that tomcat, and when he smiled he had the same feral grin, the same casual gaze that belied a killer's heart. Those eyes raked over us all now, assessing, calculating. Then he turned to the old man and said something to him in the foreign language they shared.

It seemed to me then, in some flash of understanding that children often have but cannot explain, that Momo was terrified of this man. It seemed that he had shrunk. Perhaps it was a trick of the odd light, or perhaps he cowered away. He would not look at him beyond a fleeting glance; he kept his head down, and muttered and muttered. The tall dark man answered him, loud and angry, and the conversation went back and forth. Then he turned away, and I could have sworn that Momo gave a great silent sigh of relief. The tall man, who must, I realized, be the captain of this vessel, now snapped his fingers and the man with the club held out to him the string of beads. He took this in his long rat's paws and as he walked down the line of captives he shuttled the beads from one end of the cord to the other until a goodly number were gathered on one side. He stopped at Agnes and tilted his head to one side as he looked at her, then tipped her chin upwards with one finger. In the uncanny light she seemed no more substantial than a moonbeam, the paleness of her hair and skin so white as to render her almost a ghost of herself.

I saw how she trembled, and how tears gathered, but I was proud to see she did not let them fall.

"Pretty. Good eyes." His English was heavily accented, and he seemed to be speaking it for our benefit, as if he were a villain in a play, trying to frighten us all. He turned Agnes's face to one side. "Good bones. You have done well, Momo. *Moomtaz*."

He shuttled another few beads along the string, then turned to the pigtailed crewman and rattled something out in their harsh tongue, and gave him the string with the place he had reached amongst the beads carefully marked. The man went running off. Although he was as solid as a barrel, his feet were as light on the ship's boards as a bird's, and made no sound. A few moments later he was back, bearing a leather bag, a bag that was clearly heavy by the way it bowed him over.

As soon as I saw that bag, I knew what was in it, for my hands started to itch and burn.

There was gold in the bag: and then I knew our fate was sealed.

Uncle Momo snatched the bag of gold and cradled it to his chest. Outraged by his cruel greed, I confronted him. "Shame on you! You have taken the children of Kernow and sold their souls to these devils. May that gold be a curse on you and all who touch it!"

He turned his dead eye upon me, and all I saw in it was my own reflection, horribly distorted: a small, pale boy lost in a sea of darkness.

15

CORSAIRS

I watched Uncle Momo and Mary climb back into the skiff and row away and my hatred flowed after them.

"I will come back!" I yelled after them, my eyes piercing the night to watch the dwindling form of the little boat plying its way through the black waters back to the magic isle. "I will come back, I promise you!"

My voice was lost in the night air, as if it had been swallowed up. If Uncle Momo and Mary had heard my threat, they gave no sign of it, but kept rowing steadily; and really, what response would they give to such an empty promise from a child but to laugh dismissively? I felt as if my heart had become a stone. I turned my face from Cornwall and never more looked back.

The tall man gave no sign of reaction to my words, but he watched them rowing away too, with a peculiar expression on his face. As a man I would recognize that expression as distaste, touched by contempt, but at the time I could not read it. It was Jack Five who spoke for all of us. "Who are you, sir, and whence do you come?"

A beam of moonlight briefly illuminated the dark face. "My name is Malik," he said in his accented English. "I am captain of this vessel. We come from North African coast."

Africa. The word spread out like a contagion amongst my companions. They whispered it among themselves, turning the three syllables over in their mouths wonderingly. It was a word most of them had probably never uttered before, heard only in the passing conversations of adults, and paid little attention to. *Africa*. What did it mean to any of them but to signify a place a long way away, perhaps as far in the world as anyone could go? And to go so far away, how would any of us ever return? *Africa*: it was the sound of all hope lost.

I remembered Old John's stories, of men from far away, with dark skin, shaved heads and curved swords. The image came quite clearly to me after all those "wasted" hours outside the inn, listening to Old John and his old salts spinning their tall tales. Tales of ships appearing out of the mists like ghosts, of sea battles and foreign devils who used magic against good honest Englishmen to best them in a fight, to scupper their ships and send them to the bottom of the ocean, caring only for their cargoes and the men aboard. Men they took to their far homeland to sell as slaves. And I remembered the story Old John had told me about the ships that had sailed into Penzance before I was born, of the men that had attacked the church there and borne away sixty men, women and children to sell into the markets of North Africa, never to return.

"They are pirates," I said softly. "Barbary pirates, from North Africa."

The pirate chief smiled, and his teeth glinted in the pale light. "That is right. We are from the lands of Barbary. But we not pirates. We corsairs! It is all a matter of honour, and among pirates no such thing. Corsairs have a code. We act for glory of Allah, and we sail beneath his flag."

I looked up. From the top of the tallest mast there waved a banner, but in the darkness I could not make it out. "Allah the All Merciful," I said, and did not know where the words had come from.

I could tell I had surprised him, for he blinked, and seemed thoughtful. Then he turned away from me and gave orders for the sails to be raised – or at least this seemed to be what he said, for at once the crew ran to haul on lines till great sheets of canvas flapped in the wind. Then two men set to winding up the great iron chain that brought the anchor up on deck. Soon we were moving out into the dark sea with the wind in our sails. The corsair chief now came along the line of his purchases, asking each of us what we could do and what skills we had learned in our short lives. When Jacks Five and Six told him they were fishermen he nodded with satisfaction: they would be easy to sell. Jack One was small and nimble, and had been a baker's boy, but his hands when inspected were soft and pink and the corsair clucked his tongue over them and seemed put out. Jack Four had been apprentice to a sailmaker, which made the captain smile widely: no doubt there would be

107

sailmakers in whatever port we were making for who would give a good price for him, too. Jack Two, the boy with the bulging eyes, was a farmer: he was well-muscled and hard-handed. The captain appeared delighted by him. He felt his arm muscles and exclaimed to his crew. "Perhaps galleys for you," he said cheerfully. We did not understand what this meant: Jack Two smiled uncertainly and his fish eyes bulged more than ever.

Jack Four knew better, though: "That's a warship, a galley: he means for you to be a rower in a warship."

"Is that bad?"

Jack Four looked away.

One by one the boys were taken away by the pigtailed man, I did not know where. The girls were given over into the care of the ship's cook. "Many more mouths to feed before this voyage over!" the captain said with gusto.

Which left just Jack Three and me. My companion was grey in the face with fatigue and pain and the effort of not falling down, even with an arm on my shoulder for support. The captain stood in front of us and looked us up and down. Then he pushed me abruptly to one side. The hard shove took me by surprise. I almost stumbled and fell; but fall Jack Three did, face down on the deck.

The corsair chief stood over him, hands on hips. "What matter with you? Get up!"

Jack Three tried valiantly, but it is hard to right yourself on a single leg with nothing to haul on. At last, I took pity on him and reached out a hand, and he grasped it gratefully and dragged himself upright. It was quite obvious the boy could put no weight on his right leg. Dropping to one knee, the captain pulled up the trouser, exposing the grubby bandages beneath. These he unravelled roughly, exposing the swollen, bruised flesh beneath.

The corsair muttered under his breath. Words in the harsh language sounded like swear words at the best of times, but I was sure these were such that he uttered. They included the words Momo and Mahmoud; and I knew he was angry that he had been tricked.

Jack started to talk very fast. "It will mend, sir, I know it. I'm a fast mender. When I was just a little lad of six or seven I fell from a horse and broke an arm and it was good as new in no time. In fact, I am sure it is stronger now than it was before, and so it will be with the leg, sir, I assure you."

I had never heard him say so many words and knew he was frightened for his life. As well he might be, for the corsair just stared at him. "What use you are with broken leg?"

If it were possible, Jack Three went even paler.

"Another mouth to feed," the captain mused. "Three weeks' food, and you might not even make the block."

The block? What did that mean? The only block I had heard of was the great block of wood they had placed beneath King Charles for the axe to bite into when they cut his head off in the year of my birth. Jack and I exchanged terrified glances.

"Slave block," the captain said, seeing our confusion. "In market. Where you be sold as slaves. You fetch lot of gold: ten times what I paid Momo. But for you—" He leaned in close to Jack Three and glared at him eye to eye. "I can get nothing for cripple."

He stepped back, called out *"Ya! Balid!"* and two of his man came running. He gestured with a thumb and Jack Three screamed, "No!"

He understood quicker than I what the corsair chief had ordered. He fought them every step of the way, but to no avail. They carried him to the side of the ship and with a great heave-ho lofted him into the air. He fell and vanished from our sight. But we heard the splash as he hit the surface of the waves.

I could hardly believe what I had witnessed. The corsair captain was staring out to sea, out into the void. His face was impassive. The event had not touched him at all.

Red fury surged through me. "Why did you do that? He is a human being, just like you! Except that maybe you are not human: I think you must be a demon."

His eyes travelled back to me. They looked as flat and dark and expressionless as the eyes of the sharks I had seen brought into St Ives harbour. Suddenly he swung back his hand as if he would hit me.

At that very instant, for some reason best known to itself, the little chet decided to stick its head up through the opening of my shirt.

The captain's hand lowered.

"A stowaway?"

I looked down. The kitten looked up, and I swear it grinned at me. Then with a frantic clawing the little beast levered itself up out of my shirt and leapt onto the corsair's shoulder, where it started up a loud, rumbling purr.

Was it showing courage and friendship by distracting this monstrous pirate from my outburst? Or being a traitor? I could not decide. With cats, it is often hard to tell. They always like to be sure where their next meal is coming from, and Byasen knew well enough it would not be from me.

The captain's long fingers closed around the belly of the chet. For a long moment I thought he would crush it to death, or hurl it over the side as he had Jack Three. But instead his harsh face softened and he brought the kitten down into his arms and cradled it against his chest, rubbing with his thumb that spot under its chin that is the secret place all cats love to have stroked. The chet's eyes closed to gleaming slits of ecstasy.

"Cats have many lives, and remember much. Does he have name?"

I told him, in Cornish and then in English. He nodded. "Magpie. Love glittery things. Live off misfortune of others. He fit my crew well." He handed Byasen back to me and gave me a long, assessing look. "What your name, boy?"

"Jack Seven is what they call me," I said stonily. I would keep my own name to myself.

"Jack Seven." He nodded. "*Moomtaz*. Good. Come with me."

111

The chet jumped up on to my shoulder. *Do not worry*, it said into my mind. *Just do what I say*.

The captain led us to a companionway and beneath it a wooden ladder that led down into the darkness. He launched himself down the ladder and disappeared towards the stern. I followed, heart thudding, remembering the ladder down into Da's fateful mineshaft. I hated the dark, and small spaces, and almost at once missed my footing, and jarred the next step so that the kitten chattered in annoyance on my shoulder just like his namesake. I hit solid ground – the lower deck – a moment later and could just make out the shadowy form of the corsair far ahead of me, moving at speed. I had to run to keep up with him, cannoning from side to side off the walls of the passageway with the rocking motion of the ship. Something brushed past me in the darkness then, and I felt the cat tense and dig its claws into my shoulder as it turned to look after it.

What? What is it? I asked it. But Byasen did not reply.

At the end of the passageway a door opened. The captain waited until I caught up, then ushered me into a small room lit only by the watery moonlight that came in through a single round porthole. He crossed to a desk, and there lit a single candle-lantern, which bathed the room in golden light.

It was not the only golden thing in that place. There was gold in the cabin: bags of it – in bars and coins, in minted coins and moulded ingots. I could not see any of it, but I could feel it. I thought my hands might burst into flame,

112

they itched so mightily. I rubbed them on my thighs, almost weeping at the discomfort.

"What matter, Jack? You ill? No place for sick, here."

Don't tell him you can sense the gold, the chet warned. *He won't like that. He's very possessive of his gold. Who knows why? You can't eat it.*

I stopped my rubbing and balled my fists, gritting my teeth till my jaw ached. I could not see the gold, but I knew there was a fortune inside the cabin: maybe as much as in Uncle Momo's secret cave.

"I hope I not make error," the corsair said, watching as I sweated and fought my "gift". "Have bargain for you. I lost cabin boy on voyage over. A fight with English navy in Channel. Just finished training him, so most irksome. But think you will do, with effort by both. Pleases my sense of balance that British take one boy from me, then give me another."

"I'm Cornish, not English," I muttered.

"Ha! A bit of spirit! If you prove worth during voyage, I not sell you. I keep you as crew. You share profits then, like rest. It is good offer, not the sort made every day. What say you?"

I stared at him, horrified. What a choice: to be sold as a slave, or to become a slaver myself! I found my tongue had frozen in my mouth. No words would come out. How could I answer a devil who had just murdered one of my comrades?

Just say yes, suggested a voice in my head.

"Yes," I stammered, before even realizing it.

He leant over the desk and grasped me by the hand. The touch of him was cold and smooth. It felt like shaking hands with a lizard. Or a rat.

"Excellent. So, Jack Seven, now you corsair, too! Welcome aboard the *Baraka* – in our language, *Good Fortune*."

And he laughed, and laughed.

16

CAPTIVES

That first night aboard the ship I could not sleep at all. The motion of the ship was disturbing: it rolled, it bucked and wallowed. Lying there on my pallet on the hard, wooden deck, I felt as if I were floating on an unquiet sea with nothing between me and the waves but my thin mattress of straw. Whenever I closed my eyes I was assailed by images of poor Jack Three and his pale body falling down and down through that black water, and of the things that lay beneath the waves.

I had heard all sorts of tales of the monstrous beings that inhabited the kingdom beneath the waves. Old John and Abdellah had told of merfolk and selkies, creatures neither quite human nor quite fish, but some queer hybrid of the two; of gigantic beasts that lurked in the oceans – sharks the size of whales with mouths that could swallow a cottage whole; squids that could wrap their tentacles around a ship and drag it to the bottom of the sea. I lay there and thought about Jack Three falling past them to Davy Jones's Locker on the far seabed. Down and down and down.

Never once did I think to blame the real monsters who inhabited the world above the waves: the men who were content to trade in human souls and call it "business". Of whom I was now one.

Tormented and guilty, I tossed and turned there on my little mattress, until at last I knew I would have to get up. I moved stealthily, afraid of waking the captain. But when I stepped out from behind the screen, it seemed he was already awake, and standing as if deep in thought, head down, with his back to me. Then my eyes adjusted to the light, and I saw it was not a man who stood there, but a lad, about my own age, brown-haired and raggedly dressed.

"Hello?" I said softly.

The figure turned and saw me behind him, and in that instant it changed. I swear its eyes went to fire, its mouth opened to show fangs; its skin became quite black. It screamed; I screamed. We stood there, apparently in equal terror of each other; then the figure collapsed on itself, and forming what looked like a ribbon, or a snake, slid across the wooden floor and vanished beneath the cabin's door.

I stood, staring after it, my heart thudding hard and fast. I must still be asleep, I told myself. It was a nightmare. Just a nightmare, brought on by seeing a boy my own age killed before my very eyes.

But I could feel the planks of the floor beneath my feet, cool and smooth; and could smell in the air something like a burnt coal, hot and fragrant. I reached out and touched the wooden screen behind me, my fingers playing across

116

the complex fretted carvings. It felt far too real to be something I dreamed. My mind must be playing tricks on me. Perhaps I had caught sight of the little cat only and my imagination had dragged a monster from my dreams into my mind's eye. . .

"Byasen?"

There was, of course, no reply.

I went to the door and looked under it; but there was nothing but darkness on the other side. Experimentally, I lifted the latch and pushed gently, expecting to find it locked, but to my amazement it swung open on to the dark companionway. My heart began thudding again. Was it still out here, the apparition? I looked cautiously about, but could see nothing and no one.

Then it occurred to me that I had not been locked in, which meant that now I was considered one of the crew. The sensation was a strange one. I was no longer a prisoner in any physical sense, but I could not rejoice in the fact, for I was just as much a prisoner to my fear, and my guilt.

I wondered where the rest of my comrades were, and determined that I would find out, and perhaps discover that their condition was not so bad. Then perhaps I would not feel quite so guilty. For this, a little unfairly, I blamed the chet. I knew whose voice I had heard in my head, egging me to accept the captain's offer.

You should be thanking me.

The words issued up from below. I looked down and found a pair of lambent eyes gleaming up at me.

117

There he was! So surely it had been Byasen I had seen, and only my stupid waking mind had made him look first a boy, then a monster, and finally a serpent. I breathed a sigh of relief.

"Thanking you?" I said aloud – too loudly, for my voice echoed dreadfully.

Just say it in your head, the chet told me. *I can hear you better like that. All those silly sounds that humans make when they talk: it's really just a lot of useless noise.*

Byasen: how is it that we can converse like this? Am I imagining it? Am I going mad?

The chet gave a snort of what must be cat-humour. *Mad? All humans are certainly rather strange, in a cat's eyes. No, you are neither mad nor imagining it. It has taken a while to find your range, but now that I have found it there should be no difficulty.*

Range?

Byasen twitched irritably. *I cannot easily explain it. It is like the sea going in and out of a cove, or the moon travelling the sky. One of the things that happen in the world. Dogs hear high-pitched noises and respond to different whistles, though they cannot whistle back, which is a great vexation to them. It makes some dogs very bad-tempered, as I'm sure you've noticed.*

Cats can hear some people's thoughts, and if we make a special connection with a human we can send a thought back along the same path down which it came. Though not everyone can hear what we say. Some people are very stupid, and some are deliberately deaf.

He paused, his eyes bright in the darkness, as if they had trapped all the available light and were beaming it back at me. I stared at him, my head spinning. What a strange and terrible day this had been. Would the shocks never stop coming?

You should be thanking me.

Thanking you?

For saving you.

Saving me?

There is no need to echo everything I say, stupid human. Or do you need to think about the silly words twice for them to make sense? It sighed, and I felt the huff of air it exhaled hot against my hand. *You should be thanking me because you have not been thrown overboard, or chained up in the dark like a dog, and you have somewhere warm and comfortable to sleep, unlike the others.*

The others, where are they?

The cat gave a mental shrug. *Somewhere down below. You have light and comfort, and good food. You should be thanking me for that,* it repeated.

Trust a cat, I thought to myself, to care only about such things as food and comfort. They are faithless, selfish beasts, out only for themselves.

The way Byasen's eyes changed shape – narrowing his gaze – warned me I could no longer keep my thoughts to myself. I could feel a little itch in my mind, feel him nosing around as if he were rooting out a mouse in a haystack. "Stop it!" I said aloud.

I sensed puzzled resentment from Byasen. Then he reiterated, *You should be happy. You saved me, and now I have saved you. We are safe and well: what does it matter about anyone else?*

The chet radiated a sense of satisfaction that I simply could not feel, not after seeing poor Jack Three thrown overboard like a leftover scrap. I suppose I should have gone straightways down into the depths of the ship to search for the others, but I was a coward. The day had been too strange for more darkness. So instead I made my way up on deck, just as the first rays of the sun crept over the horizon, lighting the bank of clouds behind us an angry purple-red, like a new bruise. Red sky in the morning, sailor's warning, I thought, and wondered for whom the warning might be.

On the horizon were low, dark shapes, but were they clouds, or land? As I gazed over the rail at them, a hand clapped me on the shoulder, making me jump almost out of my skin. It was the corsair captain.

"They call those islands the Scilly Isles. We put in there in a little while. Do not think to escape."

"I cannot swim," I said flatly.

He gave a little laugh. "That good. We take on fresh water, and some . . . wares. As for you, your first task is get my coffee from cook. Go fast and bring back carefully: spill a drop and you regret it! Off you go."

I was about to object that I did not know where to find the cook, when the chet butted its head against my leg. *I know where the kitchen is*, it said, and took off up the deck.

Of course it did. It had no doubt already made friends with the cook and stuffed its face with scraps from last night's meal. I followed it. Down in the kitchen, which on a ship they call the galley, I found the cook, a huge man in a long brown robe and a great white apron. He was attending to an oven that looked like the mouth of hell, for its interior glowed a bright cherry red. The smell of fresh bread wafted out of it. My stomach rumbled. I was no better than the chet, I thought ruefully. "I have come for the captain's coffee," I said loudly, and he turned. There was flour all over his face and beard. I almost laughed.

He frowned at me and said something foreign. "Coffee?" I repeated and mimed drinking something, and then made a gesture above my head to indicate the captain's onion-like turban and he laughed and nodded. "*Ka'hawa!*"

He went to the stove and took a great steaming kettle from it and set about some complex preparation. Behind him, something white moved, like a little ghost. It was Agnes, her face drawn and pinched, her eyes red from weeping.

"Agnes!" I cried, both horrified and relieved to see her. "What has he done to you?"

"Nothing, I am fine. It is Alice. She fell down in a faint last night from sheer terror, and I think she may be dead!"

My heart thudded. Little Alice dead? The very thought of another lost made my stomach clench. The image of her must have been bright in my mind, for all of a sudden the little chet said, *I will go and look for her*, and ran silently away.

"Oh, Agnes. I am so sorry."

She gave me a crooked smile. "Thank you, Jude. It warms my heart to see that you at least are well." She looked away, then whispered, "Poor Jack Three."

His name hung between us like a curse. I could think of nothing to say. We stood there, staring uncertainly at each other, thinking our thoughts, but the chet did not return, and tears were gathering in Agnes's eyes again. "Please don't cry," I said. "I'm sure she'll be all right. They wouldn't throw Alice overboard: she's worth too much money to them."

It was true: but perhaps it was not the right thing to say. The tears began to trail down her pale cheeks and I felt worse than ever. I was almost relieved when the cook brought a tall, decorated glass containing some strong-smelling black liquid. He had, I saw with dismay, filled it to the brim, and when I took it from him, my hand felt as if it were on fire and I almost dropped it. The cook stared at me, expressionless. How useful it would be, I thought, to be able to read men's minds, and not just the chet's. I could have avoided this whole situation, and saved the others too. If we had all run away from Uncle Momo down on the strand he could never have caught us all and sold us to these people. But would you want all that cruelty and unkindness in your own head?

"Goodbye, Agnes," I said softly. "I will find out what I can about Alice and come back and tell you when I can."

Then before she could answer I walked quickly away, ignoring the pain in my hand, and trying not to spill a drop. The ladder back up to the deck was a challenge, but I managed it, found the captain and handed over the horrible stuff. He sipped it and smiled. "You quicker than last. We make fine corsair out of you. Now go wash my clothes."

I hesitated.

"What is it, boy?"

"The littlest girl, Alice. I heard she was unwell—"

The blow he gave me made tears spring to my eyes. My ear rang and burned so much I heard him as if through a roaring sea: "Say no more, unless you wish join her."

Like a coward, I ran to do the washing.

We sailed due west with the sun chasing us across the sea. An hour later, we drew close to an island, sailed around its lee side and dropped anchor within the protective arm of a remote, tree-lined bay. The land did not seem far away. I could make out a row of little cottages and a squat church tower whose graveyard came right down to the dunes, but no people, though there were fishing boats drawn up on the sand, and the usual paraphernalia of nets and crab baskets and cork floats.

How I wished I could swim: there were only a hundred yards or so between the *Baraka* and the strand, but to me it might as well have been a thousand miles.

Two longboats were lowered over the side and away in them went eight of the crew, including the pigtailed man, fully armed and looking mightily fearsome. I watched them scull across the expanse of sea, draw up the boats on the beach and walk up towards the cottages. There, they disappeared from sight for a time and a little while later emerged carrying barrels, boxes and sacks, and pushing ahead of them a number of men. Two men in slouch hats and smocks and breeches tucked into top boots came out of the last cottage to watch the proceedings and, clapping the pigtailed man on the back, took from him a bag of something, and then shook hands with him, as if on a deal.

I realized with a sinking heart that it was not just devils like Uncle Momo and Mary who were profiting in this vile trade, but also my fellow countrymen, and I felt the shame creep over me like a physical sickness.

These new captives were taken at musket-point to the boats, where they were loaded in along with the barrels and boxes, just another form of merchandise. The boats were stuffed to the gunwales: water slopped over the sides as they came slowly back.

I could not tear my eyes away. Though the scene was played out by daylight, it seemed horribly familiar to me. When the longboats drew close, I saw that the men the crew had brought with them from the island all had their hands tied together with rope. Many were bruised and bloodied, some were bandaged. All looked resigned to their fate, the fight gone out of them.

As they came into the lee of the *Baraka* one of the captives looked right at me. He held my gaze for a long moment; then he spat, very deliberately, over the side. And at that moment I knew that, in his eyes at least, I had become one of the legion of the damned.

17

THE HOLD

That night I waited till the corsair captain went up on deck for his watch, took the candle-lantern from his desk, and made my way down into the chilly depths of the ship. I did not want to go there, but I was driven by need, and by guilt.

My little cat had not reappeared all the day long. I had to find out if Alice was still alive and make good on my promise to Agnes.

Down there, a further deck down from where lay the captain's cabin, the dark pressed in on me, cold and clammy. Sometimes I thought I could hear voices, but could not tell where they came from. More than once I whirled around, thinking I was being followed, but found nothing there but the dancing shadows thrown by the candle's flame. But there were other noises too, more disturbing than the sound of a human voice. Strange scratchings and groanings that might have been the creak of the ship's timbers, but I did not think they were. Were they inside the ship, or outside? On the whole I had rather they were in the sea beyond, no matter what horrors made them. A dozen times I turned to retrace my steps; a dozen times I forced myself on. Then something brushed past me, dark and catlike.

"Byasen?" I called quietly, but if it was the cat it did not answer me, either by mewing or by sending words into my head. I felt the little hairs on the back of my neck stand up one by one. With an unsteady hand, I held up the lantern.

What else could it be down here, in the bowels of the ship, but rats? Rats the size of terriers! I waved the lantern around, but all I could make out was a flick of tail and a blur of body, and bright beady eyes winking out of the nooks and crannies in which they took shelter.

It's only rats, Jude, I told myself firmly. Remember the rats in Farmer Scoble's barn? These are no worse than those, if a little bigger. I took a hold of my panic and squeezed it into the back of my mind. What was important, I reminded myself, was finding little Alice and the others. I concentrated on the ground before me and tried not to think about the rats. So I continued, head down, concentrating grimly on where I was putting my feet.

Turning a corner, I suddenly had the distinct sensation that someone had been there just before I arrived. A faint spicy smell lingered on the close air, and it seemed to me the very same smell I had sensed in the captain's cabin the night before. I thought I heard whispers, but could not make out the words. Were there crewmen down here, guarding the prisoners? The light of my lantern would alert them to my presence. I was tempted to extinguish the candle; but only for a moment. Better to see whoever was there than be plunged into terrible darkness. Better to seem lost, than creeping around like a spy. On I went, one shuffling footstep at a time, sure I was not alone, but too afraid to call out.

I came to a hatchway in the floor. I stood there, looking down at it for a long, long moment. Down there, I felt sure, lay the answers I sought. Even so, I feared to open it, though it was closed only by a sliding iron bar.

When I was very small, I had been caught by Mam going through her things in the room she slept in with my da. Beneath the bed I had found a pretty box, painted with flowers and closed with a small silver key. I could not resist opening it, and had been most disappointed to find within only some dead old flowers, a few scraps of paper and a mouldy thing wrapped in a handkerchief. These I had tipped out on to the floor, and the flowers had gone immediately to dust. Mam found me there, scraping all the fragments back in, and she let out a wail, which was most unlike her, and went down on her knees to try to save the remnants. How could I, a boy of five, understand the value she gave to the posy she had carried down the aisle when she married Da? Or to the clumsily penned love notes he had sent her; or the piece of wedding cake she had kept as good luck?

After she finished crying, she told me the story of another box, untimely opened. I do not recall all the details of it now. It was a girl, I think, with a strange foreign name.

She, like me, had found a box and been unable to resist the urge to see what was inside. And so of course she had opened it, and all manner of terrible things had flown out into the world like a cloud of black bats: envy and greed and violence and any number of wickedness. The poor silly girl had sat there with this storm of horrors streaming past her, crying out in fear, until at last the box was empty. As Mam told me this, I cried too, suddenly dreading I had done far worse than spoil a few old flowers. She had dried my face for me.

"But there was one more thing in the box," she said. "Tiny and frail-seeming, yet it was the strongest thing of all. Out it crept into the light. It perched on the edge of the box for a moment, pale and trembling; then, like a butterfly emerging from its chrysalis, it unfurled its wings and spread them wide and they were bright with colour – all the colours of the rainbow that had up till then been missing from the world – and up into the sky it beat its passage, casting joy and colour as it went. And its name was Hope, and it was the strongest force of all, strong enough to counter all the evils the girl had let out into the world."

All I had taken from the tale at the time was that you should never open things that did not belong to you, since curiosity can be a very dangerous thing indeed. But I remembered the story now, and the way Mam had smiled as she told it, and I told myself that no matter what lay beneath the cover of the hatch, there was always Hope, which would help to combat the worst things I might find.

And so I hauled the bolt back and pulled the hatch open.

A great fetid wave rose up and engulfed me: all the worst smells in the world compounded into a single powerful stench. I recoiled so fast I almost dropped the lantern, and turned and gagged and thought I would be sick.

Perhaps, I thought when the worst of the smell had passed, that was the bad stuff coming out of the box. Perhaps I could now look down into the hold and find Hope. I thought of Alice, as pale and trembling as the little creature that had perched on the side of the box in Mam's tale, and gathered my courage. I must find her; and if she were down in this dark place where giant rats ran freely, then I must somehow rescue her. Gripping the lantern tightly, I crouched and let it down a way into the hold. By its gentle golden light I was gifted a vision of Hell.

I had thought I might find my erstwhile companions down there, sitting in the darkness, shut in as we had been in Momo's back room, along with the men we had picked up that morning from the Isles of Scilly. But I had not expected what I saw. Row upon row of suffering people, their faces upturned like flowers seeking the sun, were bound together by cuffs and chains, by fetters and iron bars, all in a squalid dark place. Men and women. Boys and girls. There must have been dozens of them down there. To my horrified eyes in that moment they all looked the same, as if fifty or more individuals could be lumped together into a single creature whose name was Slave. And in that same moment, I knew, though it was selfish and wrong, that I would do anything to avoid joining them. Whatever that might take.

The moment of revulsion which had separated me so far from them passed and my gaze refocused. I was able to make out the faces of Jacks Two and Five, and some of the men who had been taken that morning from the island. My eyes swept over them, searching for little Alice, but of her there was no sign.

"Have you brought food?" someone called out hopefully.

"I'm sorry, no. I am looking for a little girl whose name is Alice, though she is sometimes called Jill."

There was much murmuring at this. Then, "What do you want with her?" a man called; and "Show your face!" came a woman's voice.

Slowly, I brought the lantern up so that it shone upon me.

"Shame on you, Jack Seven!" shouted the boy with the fish eyes, whom I had known as Jack Two. "Why are you out there while we are imprisoned in this hell?"

"I do not know," I said truthfully. "The captain decided to make me his servant. Are you all down there? All the Jacks, and little Alice too?"

"We're all down here. We haven't seen Jack Three or the girls. What news of them?"

I looked away. "They threw Jack Three overboard because of his leg. Agnes is helping in the kitchen, but her little sister fell down in a faint, and I'm looking for her."

"So that's the only reason you've come down here," Jack

Two said angrily. "It's your fault Jack Three got hurt, not that you give a damn. I might have known you wouldn't care twopence for the rest of us. You always spent your time hanging around with those floss-headed poppets, as if the rest of us weren't good enough for you."

The unfairness of this stung me. "That's not true! If I could help you, I would."

"Bring us the keys to these locks, then!" another voice – a man – cried. "You're the only one out there who's not one of these foreign devils. Find us the keys to these fetters. We are weak, but if we can free ourselves we can work together to take this ship!"

"I do not know where the keys are kept."

"You are our only hope!" cried a woman. "Only you can save us!"

Oh no: what was this madness? How could I help? I was just a boy, and a prisoner as surely as they were, even though my current living conditions might be rather better.

"Yes, Jack Seven, only you can save us!" echoed Jack Two, and it seemed to me that his voice was mocking.

"Take pity on us!" shouted a man, rattling the chains that held him. "We are just poor fishermen taken from our vessels while trying to do an honest day's work to keep our families from starving. What will the little ones do without me, without all their fathers, and the little bit of income and fish we bring home? It is not just for our souls that I beg you. It is for the sake of our families – good Cornish folk just like you!"

"Cornish!" Another man spat out the word with venom. His accent was foreign. "Cornish as bad as these devils. They draw our ship on rocks using false lights and wreck us. Half crew drowned. Then they steal our cargo, take rest prisoner, sell us to slavers."

I listened with horror. Of course I knew about the wreckers – who in Cornwall did not? And had not my own family profited from the cargoes of ships washed up on our rocky coast? I felt sick. Why was the world such a confusing place? Why couldn't people be clearly marked out as good or bad, so that all knew who was who and could choose to keep company with those like themselves, and avoid the rest? The Cornish and Scillonians should be good folk. Uncle Momo, Mary and the pirates were clearly evil. But Momo had first appeared to me as a kind old man, despite his weird glass eye, so what did I know? How I wished that Mam had bequeathed me the gift of finding the gold in a man's soul rather than the cold yellow ore that caused such grief in the world.

"Not all the Cornish are bad," I said quietly. "They are not all wreckers or thieves."

They all stared up at me expectantly, like a nestful of baby birds awaiting the arrival of a parent bearing worms, their pleading eyes open as wide as avid mouths. Suddenly it seemed that everything was down to me.

"I will find the keys," I promised.

Then I closed the hatch quickly and turned away, my heart beating fast. What had I done?

Pandora. The name flew suddenly into my head. It was Pandora who had opened the forbidden box. But unlike Pandora, I had found no Hope waiting for me in the bottom of mine.

As I made my way back above-decks, I was suddenly struck by the unpleasant feeling that I might be that Hope, for the poor souls locked below.

18

THE CAT'S STORY

Did I set out at once to search for the keys that would set my fellow prisoners free? I am ashamed to say I did not. Instead I retraced my steps and went straightways back to the captain's cabin, my head full of horror and fear.

The chet was waiting for me there.

Where have you been? it said crossly just as I asked the same question.

I have a lot to tell you, we both chorused.

This is the tale that Byasen told me, though I have had to use some of my own words in places, where he put only pictures in my head.

I went to look for the small female, as I told you when I left you in the Place of Food. I thought she would smell like her littermate (*by this I think he meant her sister Agnes*) so I picked up that scent and followed it. First it took me up to the top deck, but then that scent grew too faint, so I went back down and quartered the ground till I picked it up again. I passed

135

the Place of Food, and the Place of Guns, and the Place of Sacks and Stores, and came to another level of the ship.

It was dark down there, but you know a cat's eyes can work well with the merest glimmer of light. I ran on with my nose to the ground, intent on the trail, for the small one's scent was unwavering. Too intent, for it meant I did not stay alert and the next thing I knew there was something right in front of me. I almost ran into it.

At first – and I know this will sound as if I have the wits of a sunstruck dog – I thought it was a giant cat. But when I blinked, it changed into a human. But it was a very odd sort of human, for I could see through it – no, don't interrupt! – I could see right through it to the darkness beyond. I stared at it so hard I could even make out the grain of the wood in the planking behind it.

"Are you a phantom?" I asked. The spirits of cats pass into new cats, but the human spirit sometimes returns after death and walks its favourite paths for a time.

"No," it said. Though the word it actually said was *Laa*, but I knew it for *No*.

"Then what are you?" I asked. And all the hairs down my spine started to stand on end the way they do when I am afraid, or about to get into a fight. Not that I was afraid, of course: not a bit of it!

Then it said a word I did not understand at all, and immediately started to dwindle. And then it scurried away like the biggest rat you ever saw. And I stood there staring after it, unable to believe my eyes.

Well, I almost turned back then and gave up on the idea of looking for the small female, but I knew you and the other one would be upset if I did not find her and so I carried on, very bravely, I thought, given the circumstances. This time I kept my head well up so that nothing could take me by surprise again. After a while her scent suddenly got much stronger, as if someone had carried her that far, then put her down, maybe to open a door. For suddenly I found myself by . . . a door. It was ajar, and there was light within. So I pushed with my head and managed to squeeze myself inside. And I found her! Yes, I found the little pale one. She was lying asleep on a fat straw mat on the floor and there was a big male human in the room. He was tall and dark, with a lot of black fur on his face— A beard? Oh, that's what it's called. He was sitting holding a thing that he was looking at very carefully. It was brown on the outside and smelled of cow, and the inside was pale and smelled of goat, and there were black squiggles all over it, like a thousand baby slugs that have come out after rain.

What? A book? And you do what with it? That makes no sense to me. Why would anyone pay such attention to something that cannot run away? Something you cannot eat. Humans are very strange sometimes.

Anyway, he was looking at it so hard he did not notice me. I slipped past him and went right up to the little female and patted her once on the cheek. (While we're talking like this, can I ask why it is that some humans have no fur on them while others have it all over their faces, but nowhere else? Oh, where else do they have fur? No need to be impatient, we will talk about this again. All I can say is it seems to me that humans are very defective cats.)

So, I patted her on the cheek, very gently, claws in, and she opened her eyes. They are very bright, her eyes, aren't they? They flared very blue and then as they adjusted to the light they went quite dark. And then she looked at me and they went very wide. She was going to say something, I could tell, so I tapped her lightly on the mouth to say *don't*, and her eyes went very round and she smiled hugely. I let her pat me a bit, but moved away before my purr started up, because you know how loud *that* can be, and then I said to her that I would tell you and her littermate, oh all right, sister, she was still alive, and then I ran away and came quickly back to the cabin to tell you, but you weren't here.

Cat, I said, after this long tale. *I have something very important to ask you. That thing you saw. What do you think it was?*

The chet gave me a long, unblinking look. *Nothing that came from our world.*

What did it mean by that? I wanted to tell Byasen what I had seen, but I hesitated. His own experience had been most strange, though mine seemed even stranger. But what did it matter if the chet thought me mad — or as crazed as a sunstruck dog? The ways that people and cats viewed the world varied enough as it was, I reasoned.

Byasen, I had a similar encounter. And I told him what I had seen in the captain's cabin, leaving nothing out, describing the creature's transformation from human, to fiery-eyed monster, to slithering serpent, even detailing the smell it had left behind.

The chet's eyes flashed. *That smell! Like something that has been in the fire but has not quite burned down to a cinder. Pepper, too, and spicy, as in the Place of Food.*

I nodded. *The one I saw was standing right over there.* I walked to where it had been but saw nothing there. I moved on round the cabin, my palms beginning to itch the further to the right I went. At last, my hands itched uncontrollably. I looked down. There was a rug there, thick and brightly coloured, with patterns of black and white and ochre set against a rich background of red. I had seen one like it once in the market with Mam. "Look at that fine Turkey rug," she had breathed, running a hand over its soft, warm wool. I had never seen her look at anything with such admiration, except, perhaps, Da. "It's come from halfway across the world and is worth a small fortune." And then she had taken her hand away from it before it cast any more magic over her, and walked quickly away.

I pulled the captain's rug back. Underneath it was a hole that had been cut into the floor, and inside the hole sat a great wooden chest, bound with iron bands and studded with iron rivets, locked by a great iron lock. Any boy in the presence of such treasure would, I am sure, set about trying to open it. But I just shuddered. Gold held no attraction for me: I knew it to be cursed.

It must have been drawn here by the gold.

Perhaps it could smell it, like you can.

I do not smell *gold. I . . . sense it.*

Well, perhaps it sensed it, too. Perhaps you and the monster are not so different after all. It paused, as if thinking about this. Then it said, *I have heard of beings that are attracted by precious metals. Fey creatures.*

Fey creatures?

Like the knockers.

My heart sank. I knew well what knockers are, the spiky black creatures which toil away beneath the ground, seeking out seams of silver and gold, tapping and knocking with their little shovels and picks. Some said they were the spirits of souls who were trapped between Heaven and Hell, unable to get into either. At once I was back in the cold, narrow adit in Da's mine where I had found the lode of gold which had brought about his death. I remembered setting the old pickaxe down there as Da told me to do, to keep them away from it when we left for the night.

But the knockers are Cornish creatures who live deep under the ground. Why would they be on a ship, and a foreign one at that?

The chet gave a mental shrug. *Don't ask me.* Then it tensed and its ears pricked up and swivelled. *Quickly! Cover up the box. I can hear the captain coming back!*

I pushed the rug back over the chest and ran back

140

towards my bed, but the door opened before I got there. In came the corsair.

"Still awake? And little Magpie, too. *Mezian!* Have work for you." Quick as a snake he had grabbed up Byasen. Then he turned to me. "You go to galley, boy. Tell cook heat up fish stew he made me. Bring bread to eat it with. Now, little cat must be a warrior."

That didn't sound good.

"Rats," the captain said succinctly. "Lower decks running with them. Massive ones, crew say. Cats natural hunters. Even a small one like this." He gave the chet a hard squeeze and I saw its eyes bulge, though whether out of pain or fear, I did not know.

I don't think it's rats down there, I warned Byasen. *I think it's the creatures we've both seen. Please don't try to take them on!*

The chet gave a bitter laugh. *There's little chance of that. Take care, Byasen.*

As I turned to leave I heard the captain calling for the pigtailed man to take him away. As he passed me in the corridor outside the cabin and looked at me with his cold, cruel eyes, I wondered whether I would ever see my chet again.

19

A PLAN

I have to admit I stole a little of the fish stew on my way back from the galley. I was feeling particularly cheered by having been able to pass on the good news about Alice to Agnes. Her smile stayed with me still. I cupped the hot bowl in the crook of my arm, and it poured its warmth into me. I was suddenly full of optimism. I was sure the chet would be fine – for the apparitions had offered neither of us violence – and if I was a true "finder", as Mam had prophesied, surely I would find the keys that would set the prisoners free.

The soupy stew smelled so good that I could not resist it, and it tasted even more delicious than it smelled. Fragrant and spicy, the fish was succulent and slippery in my mouth. It left a searing sensation along the side of my tongue.

Unfortunately it also left telltale golden traces on my fingers, as the captain noticed when I handed the bread and bowl to him. He took them from me, turned and placed them carefully on the desk behind him, then fetched me such a clout about the head that my ears rang and I saw stars.

"Little thief! Saffron not for slaves! Do you know how much costs an ounce of saffron? More than its weight in gold! And do you know what I do to any that steal gold from me?"

I shook my head, which made the blood rush and pound most painfully.

"String them up from yardarm and slit open bellies for flies and scavenging birds to feast on!" He glared at me so ferociously that I felt sure this would be my fate. I felt it so acutely that I could imagine the cold edge of his knife across my poor, hot skin.

Gold again, I thought. I remembered the saffron that Mam used in the cakes that came out of the oven like bars of sunlight. I remembered how she took me out along the cliff to her secret place where she had planted the little bulbs in a sunny aspect and showed me the crocus flowers that had sprouted there. Creamy white and violet-blue and egg-yolk yellow, they poked their heads up through the cold autumn earth long after most of the other plants had gone away. "See how brave they are?" she said. "They do not fear the cold or the future, for they carry their own fire within. Crocuses came to our shores in ancient times, like cats and magic, brought by the Phoenicians."

She would leave the flowers to bloom for a few days so that their corms might get their fill of sun, before harvesting them. From inside the petals she would pull the delicate red stamens, and lay them out in long lines on a piece of linen to dry in the loft and become saffron. Last year's crop was probably still up there. But I would never taste it in any of Mam's lovely saffron cake again. The thought made my eyes prick with tears.

"Yes, boy. Be afraid. Be very afraid. Sometimes we bastinado the wrongdoer first. Do you know what bastinado means?" He thrust his face at me.

I blinked the tears away and said no, very short.

"Hang them up and beat soles of feet, fifty or hundred times, with hard stick. After that some never walk again. But that not matter. We just carry them to gibbet!"

I could tell he was used to terrorizing people like this, and that he enjoyed it. Oddly, this realization put some backbone in me. He has given me two strong blows, I said to myself: but he shall never give me more! And thus my resolve to find the keys and release the prisoners was further hardened.

All that morning I went about the ship as if I had three pairs of eyes, not just one. At midday I went to the galley.

"Agnes," I said softly while the cook was in the storeroom. "Have you seen a man carrying a big bunch of keys?" I knew that members of the crew made their way down here by ones and twos throughout the day, whenever they could escape their deck tasks, to beg a bit of bread or a glass of the sweet tea the cook kept constantly on the brew.

She shook her head. "I've been too worried about Alice to take much notice of anything. Why?"

The cook was coming back, but I was pretty sure he spoke no English. "For the prisoners. To release them."

Her eyes widened. "Jude——!"

I put a finger to my lips. "They must feed the captives sometimes."

She nodded, frightened. "Early in the morning, then again when the sun goes down."

I grinned, devil-may-care. "I'll be back just before sunset."

I went about my duties with an energy and willingness that took the corsair captain by surprise, especially after his earlier rough treatment of me. I could feel his eyes boring into my back as I swept and scrubbed his cabin till every corner of it gleamed.

"Good," he said, rubbing his hands. "Good servant. Cat eager, too. He jump right out of first mate's hands down there in dark, so eager is he to kill rats."

That's what you think, I thought. I felt guilty. I had barely given the chet a thought all that long day, so taken up was I with my heroic plan. As soon as I was alone, I sent out a questing thought.

Byasen?

His response came faintly, as if from afar. It felt like a tickle in my head, a sort of question mark, like the shape his tail made when he ran towards me.

Relief made me tremble. *Oh, Byasen, I am so sorry. Are you all right?*

I am still alive. If you even care.

145

I do care. It's just. . . It's complicated. Where are you?

I have no idea. It's dark and damp and cold.

No rats?

His reply was filled with contempt. *Of course there are rats. There are always rats. We have made a bargain between us. I will leave them alone if they leave me alone.*

What about the . . . the other things?

A pause. *They are here, too. We have made a different sort of bargain.*

Are you safe? Have they hurt you?

I waited, but no reply came. As the day wore on I called him again and again in my mind, but no matter how hard I tried he did not respond. I did not know whether it was because he was angry with me, and shutting me out, or whether something had happened to him. I thought of the "bargain" he had made with the rats and decided he was too clever for that. I looked out of the porthole and saw that the sun was starting to dip towards the sea. Well, now it was my turn to be clever.

When I entered the galley, Agnes looked startled. "Be careful, Jude," she started to say. Behind me a harsh voice barked out orders and the cook came running.

It was the pigtailed man. The look he turned on me was unfriendly. "Why you here?" he asked brusquely.

I decided to brazen it out. "I'm here to help," I said brightly. "I've finished all my other tasks and the captain sent me to help carry food down to the captives."

His beady eyes narrowed as if he did not believe a word of it, and my heart started to hammer. Not too late to back out, came a little voice in my head; my own, I think, though now I sometimes wonder whether it was the chet's. But then the man threw his head back and laughed. "Malik know what hurts. Prisoners see you. Know there is no hope. They think you traitor."

He turned to the man accompanying him, a portly fellow in a stained tunic, with nasty yellowed toenails as long as claws, and translated what he had said, and they laughed together.

"Little turn-shirt!"

Turncoat, I corrected in my mind, deciding, probably wisely, not to correct him out loud. The captain might be ready to deal out a blow from an open hand, but this one looked as if he'd as soon skewer me with his curved sword, or with the sharp little dagger he carried bound to his chest.

"You carry bread." He took a sack from the cook and tossed it to me with such force it almost sent me flying. When he took a step back to let the other man pass, I heard something jangle: a rich, clanking sound. Pretending to concentrate on getting the sack over my shoulder, I sneaked a good look.

Yes! The keys!

They were there, at his belt, right beside his pistol. By heavens, he was well armed. Any plan I contemplated had not, stupidly, involved pistols and swords. . .

147

There was a dragging sound, and I saw the second man, much slighter than the first mate, desperately trying to heft a huge copper pot with a ladle stuck in it, off the stove. He got it into his arms and staggered under its weight. It smelled awful, almost as bad as the porridgy stuff Mary had given us. I could not help but peer into it as he passed me. In it, I could make out fins and tails, and a bobbing fish's head. No doubt all the leavings after the cook had used the good flesh in the saffron-flavoured stew for the captain.

As I turned to follow him Agnes crossed her fingers for me. She looked terrified.

Down we went, down into the darkness. The two crewmen were so used to this vessel in which they ate and slept and breathed that they seemed to know every knot of wood, every rib and rivet of it. They took no lantern, but moved confidently in the pitch-black of the lower deck, as if they were strolling along a sunlit beach, and I stumbled along behind them, trying not to fall flat on my face. At one point something brushed past my feet.

Byasen?

No reply. Perhaps it had been a rat, after all. I shuddered.

When we reached the hatch I had found the day before, the pigtailed man bent and unlatched it and we all descended into that awful place. I was no sooner down than they started.

"Traitor!"

"Judas!" Which sounded so close to my own name, I almost answered to it.

"Gone over to the enemy, have you, boy?" cried one of the men who had been taken from the island.

I was about to protest but he gave me a wink, which I recognized by a long moment of darkness flicking over the sheen of his eye, and then I knew they were doing it as pretence, to cover for the one they thought might save them. It seemed to work. The first mate laughed as he undid the locked bar on the first row of captives, freeing their hands so they could eat, seeming to enjoy their taunts, but they soon quietened as the food came by. I watched as they cupped their hands, eager for the horrid sludge containing the fish heads and tails and fins; watched as they plunged their faces into the horrid stuff and snaffled it up like starving animals, without bowl or spoon. I followed with the bread, trying not to watch with fascination.

"We're counting on you, Jack," a woman whispered as I came to her.

I looked at her queasily, but I doubted she could see the uncertainty in my face, for I could feel the warmth of her smile through the darkness.

Shielded by the pot-man's back, Jack Two grinned at me, his teeth as white as pearls. "Soon!" he whispered cheerfully.

They all had such faith in me. To them I was Hope in the Darkness. But what could I do against two armed men?

Along each row we made our way, wading ankle-deep through the bilge-water and filth. The first mate kept a close fist on the keys throughout the unlocking, the feeding, the locking again. I darted a glance at the big iron ladle. Could I snatch it out of the pot and knock him over the head with it? Certainly it was heavy enough to lay him out cold. But could I bring myself to such violence, and if I could and by some miracle it worked, how would I fend off the other man? It was all too impossible. I trudged along, feeling unmentionable horrors squidging between my toes.

At last we finished the rounds and made our way back to the ladder. Was this the end of my so-called plan? My head felt empty of ideas. I had failed. They sent me up first, as if making sure I could not conspire without them. Up I went, hand over hand, and waited in the companionway, defeated and alone.

Or so I thought.

The pot-man came up next, bearing the huge copper vessel with the ladle rattling around inside. For a moment my hands itched the way they did in the presence of gold. I could almost feel myself reaching out for it and dealing him such a blow that he would fall and take the other man with him. But I could not do it. It seemed I was no hero, after all.

The pot-man pushed past me rudely. I was in his way and he let me know it. Now the first mate's shaved skull came into view, followed by his odd topknot. He reached the top of the ladder and had just started to shift his weight on to the solid floor when a shape darker even than the surrounding gloom detached itself from the shadows and shot between his legs, taking his feet from under him. His hands clawed for a hold and found nothing. For a moment he hung there in space, his mouth a black hole in his face; then he fell with an echoing cry back down into the hold, landing with a great thud and a splash.

For a second, there was silence. Then the prisoners began to shout and jeer. There came a voice in my head. *Now's your chance, Jude.*

I looked around, and saw a silvery gleam. *Clever Byasen!*

Well, hurry up: get down there and get those iron things you keep thinking about. Don't hang about!

It was now or never. The second man was shouting out something to the fallen man, but he gave back no reply. I nipped on to the ladder. "I'll go and help him!" I said brightly, not for the benefit of the pot-man, who spoke no English, but in case the first mate was still conscious.

He wasn't. I shook him, and he made no response.

"Give me his dagger," the man nearest me whispered. "Quickly!"

Fumbling, I pulled the thin silver blade from the scabbard on the mate's chest and passed it to him. His teeth gleamed in the darkness as he grinned.

"Now the keys!"

These proved more difficult, for they were attached to his belt by a clip of iron and he was half lying upon them.

It took a lot of effort to move him. I had no idea a man could be so heavy. Then it took an eternity to open the clip and drag the keys off. They clanked and scraped loudly to pronounce my guilt and I sensed the pot-man staring down at me, trying to see through the gloom what I was doing. I glanced upwards and saw that he was about to throw a leg over the ladder. Just then the pigtailed man let out a horrifying groan.

"He's alive!" I shouted in mock joy, but now the pot-man was starting to descend.

Swiftly, desperately, I thrust the keys down inside my shirt. They lay cold as a knife blade against the hot skin of my belly, and for a moment I remembered the captain's boast of hanging thieves from the yardarm and slitting them open. My pulse began to race, faster and faster, as the first mate hauled himself upright. I was sure that the thudding of my heart against my ribs would make the keys jump and jangle and give me away.

Words began to pour out of the injured man, harsh words that flew around the enclosed space of the hold like angry bats in a cave. I saw his hands dark against the pallor of his shirt, patting, searching. . .

He found the empty scabbard, and roared; then found the keys gone too. Sweeping his hands through the dirty water around him, he came up with nothing. He stared at me, the whites showing all round his pupils like the eyes of a maddened bull. "Where are they?"

I found I could say nothing, for panic stopped my throat.

He seized me by the arms and shook me so hard my teeth rattled. Unfortunately, that was not all that rattled. . .

The keys. . .

At that moment the man with the dagger made his move. There was a sudden movement, followed by a cry. I heard chains rattle, and an English curse. He had nicked the pigtailed man's arm, but with his hands fettered, the captive had been unable to get any force behind the blow. A dark wet line showed through the first mate's white sleeve: he was wounded, but the wound was severe enough only to madden him further. Drawing his curved sword with a flourish he swung it through the black air.

I was lucky: I was just out of his range. But the man with the dagger was not. Like a silver moonbeam, the blade split the darkness, and took his head right off at the neck.

There was barely any light down there in the hold to illuminate this vile murder, but still we all screamed. I had not known any more about the man who was killed than that he was a captive and had a West Country accent, but even so I did not want to see his blood fountaining up from the red stump of his neck, or his severed head rolling gracelessly in the filth, his sightless eyes glimmering with their death stare. All this, I imagined, and worse.

The first mate wiped his sword on the dead man's shirt and sheathed it. Then, suddenly, the world was upside down. Holding me hard by my ankles, the pigtailed man shook me violently, and the keys slithered from my belly, down my chest, then along my neck, and fell with a splash into the bilge-water. At once, the man dropped me on my head in a painful heap, fished them out and held them up triumphantly.

"Stupid child! You will regret this!"

He bent and unlocked the bars to which the dead man's fetters were attached, shoved the corpse to one side and pushed me down in his place. He tightened the iron bonds around my wrists and ankles and locked the bars again. Then he retrieved the dagger from the dead man's hand and waved it in front of my nose.

"Tomorrow at dawn we hang you," he spat at me. "With this blade I slit your belly open so the sea eagles feed on you."

20

DJINN

I sat there in the darkness, with hands and feet fettered in iron, and my head in my hands. At first I wept. I could not help it. I wept for fear of the imminent end – and a horrible end at that – to my poor, short life, and for the man who had died right in front of me, who lay there still, with his head lying somewhere else.

"Don't cry, lad," said one of the women at the sound of my sobs. "You did your best."

"Take heart," growled a gruff voice behind me. A chain clanked and a hand rested briefly on my shoulder. "You tried and we all thank you for that. It was brave of you."

The human touch and the sympathy in his voice made the tears flow even harder, to my shame. Now all sorts of folk were calling out to me:

"Perhaps it won't come to a hanging. They've already lost the price of one man. Why lose another?"

"Two, you mean. There was the lad with the broken foot. Their investment's diminishing all the time."

But others disagreed. "They'll want their revenge,"

155

said one man gloomily. "They'll call it 'honour', the scum."

"And to discourage the rest of us from trying anything."

None of this gave me comfort. There came a long period of quiet in which one by one they slept, upright on the hard benches, jammed against one another; someone even snored. There was no chance of my sleeping, for my mind was in uproar at the thought of this being my last few hours. But I was dog-weary, and sometimes my thoughts wandered and sometimes I drifted in and out of slumber and jerked suddenly upright. It was in this state – neither quite asleep, nor quite awake – that I heard the voice.

First of all it said something in a language I could not comprehend. It sounded like *Maa trahv'sh*. Then it said, *N'avez pas peur*. At that time in my life I spoke neither Arabic nor French, so still I did not understand. At last, the voice said, into my mind, *Do not be afraid*. And then, as if to make a nonsense of this advice, a shape started to materialize in the dark air before my eyes. At first it looked like a twist of flame, a bright, orange, living thing. Then it steadily took on shape and substance, until a little girl with hair like a fiery halo stood in front of me.

She smiled at me, and her eyes were made of flame.

I was too frightened even to cry out. Too frightened to look away. As I watched, the figure wavered, became paler and slighter. It took on the appearance first of Agnes, then, shrinking further, of little Alice.

What horrible magic was this?

"Who are you?" I whispered aloud when I finally managed to command my voice.

Speak in your head, the thing said without moving its mouth, the flames dancing in its eyes. *As you do with the cat.*

So it knew about Byasen. And it knew Alice. Had this thing found the little girl and stolen her form? Was her homeless spirit wandering somewhere above me in the ship? Was she dead? Or worse, possessed?

What have you done with Alice? I questioned it.

It made a puzzled face. *Done with her? I have done nothing with her.*

Then why do you look like her?

To please you, so that you are not afraid. I saw her sleeping. A pretty child.

The way it said this – *child* – suggested to me that however it appeared to me now, this thing was no child itself. In fact, I had the sense that it was old: very old, even ancient. And it brought with it that musty, burned smell I had smelled in the captain's cabin when I saw the boy/monster/serpent. The smell Byasen had reported, too.

What are you? I tried again.

My name is Zaafran. It means "saffron" in your tongue. I am of the tribe of the Banou No'man, of the kingdom of the djinn.

Djinn. The word stirred a memory buried deep in the back of my mind. A memory that was powerfully associated

157

with a taste of sugar, a taste so sweet it made my mouth water. Sugar! We rarely had any in the cottage, for it was very expensive. So where had I tasted sugar and heard this strange word? I rummaged after it and came up, quite suddenly, with a memory of sitting at the feet of Old John the sailor, outside the inn, and hearing his friend Abdellah — who claimed he had once been a Barbary pirate — speak of these things he called "djinns". But what were they? I recalled, dimly, his tales of magic and trickery, but they brought me no nearer to understanding what I was dealing with here.

What is a djinn?

It looked surprised that I should ask such a simple thing. It looked as if everyone should know. Perhaps, wherever it came from, everyone did.

We are the beings of smokeless flame. We were among the first beings in the world. We were made before human beings, before animals and trees and fishes, when there was just rock and water. It says so in the Holy Book, and there you will find us.

I stared at it, nonplussed. I have to admit, with a certain shame, that I did not know my Bible well, nor, at that ignorant time in my life, did I realize that there were other holy books. I said, *Are you . . . angels?*

Peals of laughter sounded in my head. *Ah, no, we are many things, but never angels.*

Demons, then? I asked, emboldened.

It cocked its head at me and I saw its face shimmer for a

moment as if it were about to reveal another version of itself.

Some may call us demons, but we are closer to you than you think, in all manner of ways. We live beside and among human beings, eating their food, sharing their fire and their shelter, and sometimes their ships.

It scowled, the expression roiling over it like smoke, distorting Alice's delicate features.

We are the wanderers, you see, nomads among djinn; always on the move, always seeking. That is our curse, laid on us by another. It is a curse we strive to lift. That is why I am here. To offer you a bargain.

Another bargain. The last one had not worked out too well. I waited.

We spoke with the cat, the djinn went on. *Or rather, the cat spoke with us. It seemed to fear for its life.* The creature grinned, showing me a set of long, sharp fangs that had no place in Alice's rosebud mouth. *It told us you have a particular gift. One that might be very useful to us.*

A speck of understanding lit inside my skull. Ah, the gold. . .

Indeed, the gold.

I grimaced. Like Byasen, it seemed the thing could read my thoughts. I hoped it could not read them all. *Was it you I saw in the captain's cabin?*

The apparition closed Alice's lips over its horrid teeth. *That wasn't me, it was Nouh.*

The air between us shimmered and the creature took on

the form of the boy I had seen that night, then resolved itself back into Alice again. It was most unnerving. I wondered, briefly, if I dreamed.

Why was he there?

The djinn's eyes narrowed. *I think you know.*

It was the gold, wasn't it? The corsair's hoard. The creature gave a little hiss but said no more. I went on, *But he could not find it, could he? That's why you need me.*

We would find it, eventually. There is something else.

I remembered, abruptly, how Da had told me to leave my pickaxe in the mine when we found the lode of ore to keep the knockers away. I raised my hands and reached out towards the creature, and it flowed away from me, losing all shape in its alarm.

It's the iron! You can't go near the corsair's treasure chest because it's wrapped with iron!

The djinn gradually regained Alice's shape, though it kept its distance. *Iron is poisonous to our kind, it's true. Its touch burns. It kills our magic. The corsairs know that, so they always guard their gold with iron.*

So you need me to find the chest and remove the gold for you. I wondered if it knew I had already located the captain's treasure chest.

We know that gold holds no sway over you, Jude Lanyon. You are rare among men. There is no one else we could trust.

And in exchange for my promise to do this?

We will save you.

They say they will kill me at dawn. There is not much time.

160

The djinn made a sort of shrug. *Time means nothing to our kind.*

Well, it means a lot to me, I said firmly.

Will you take the bargain?

It should have been a simple answer, for Death was staring me in the face. But something made me uneasy. I wondered for a passing moment what such beings wanted with cold yellow ore and decided they were like magpies, attracted by glitter and gleam. But still there was something that itched away at me, a question I could not quite frame. Say yes, I urged myself. Dawn would be coming soon, and with it my execution! There was no point in refusing this offer of help, no matter how bizarre the source, except that to trade with demons surely damned my soul to Hell. But I doubted very much that I was bound for Heaven anyway. I sighed.

I will do it.

The djinn grinned, showing just the tips of its fangs, which suddenly looked to me a lot like a cat's. *I believe in your country you shake hands to seal a deal. But I am sorry that is not possible while you wear those fetters. I will take your word as your bond.*

Now the Alice-shape dissipated and in its place came a great black storm cloud that towered over me, roiling and writhing until at last it took the form of a giant man whose turbaned head brushed the ceiling of the hold. A black beard curled over its white robe; silver earrings hung from its ears; golden bracelets shone upon its wrists. It looked like a bigger, richer version of the corsair chief. Except that I could see the dark planks of the ship through it. And its eyes were full of fire.

In a booming voice it intoned, *But I warn you, Jude Lanyon, if you fail to deliver your promise you will forfeit your soul. There will be no escape for you, in the waking world or in your dreams. Djinns never forget a broken promise, and none can match us for vengeance. We can fly, we can cross water; we can traverse every divide. Even death will not save you from us.*

"I believe you," I said. And I did.

As I spoke these words, the djinn flowed upwards towards the ceiling, becoming a streaming ribbon of fire which licked around the edge of the hatch and disappeared from view. I sat there staring after it, blinking my eyes in the darkness.

"What?" said a man. "What do you believe, lad?"

"The djinn," I said, the shock of the encounter making me unwary. "I believe the djinn when he says they will take my soul."

"The lad is rambling, poor little chap," came a woman's sympathetic voice.

"Dreaming, more like, Susan," said the man.

"Who can blame him?" said another. "On his last night on earth, it is good to dream."

"Hush!" whispered Susan. "He'll hear you."

"Did you not see it?" I cried.

"See what, lad?"

162

"The djinn — the being of smokeless flame. He took the form of little Alice, but his eyes were aglow with fire, and his teeth were as sharp as a cat's. . . Did you not see him? At first he was as small as a child, but in the end he was as tall as a pillar. He said his name was Zaff . . . Saffron. . ." I stumbled over the word, realizing how unlikely this sounded; how probable it was that I had created a figment, a thing drawn from my imagination.

"Lost his wits, poor soul. The fear, I expect."

They muttered like this amongst themselves for a long time and after a while, I began to believe that I had indeed only dreamed the strange being and its unlikely bargain. I felt certain that my wits were addled by fear and that there was no hope of rescue.

I waited and waited, and soon the air in the hold turned a barely perceptible lighter shade of grey and I knew that somewhere outside the ship, the sun had risen. And still the djinns did not come.

Then at last I heard the sound of footsteps overhead. The hatch creaked open. Four figures peered in. One held a lantern, and it was by the golden glow of its light that I made out with a sinking heart the forms of the corsair captain, the pigtailed man and two other crewmen.

They had come to take me away and hang me.

That morning the cabin boy known as Jack Seven, or sometimes as Jude Lanyon of Kenidjack, was taken up from the hold of the corsair vessel *Baraka*, and with very little

163

ceremony was hanged — not by his beaten feet as the captain had threatened, but by his neck, till he was dead.

After that — though the first mate drew his cruel, curved sword, its blade as sharp and silver as a sickle moon, intent on fulfilling his promise to slit the boy open and let scavenging birds feed on his entrails — the body was cut down and dropped over the side into the deep blue sea.

What no one relates — perhaps because, the entertainment over, no one bothered to witness it — was that the corpse, most peculiarly, made no splash.

21

A TRICK

So let me tell you how I come to be relating this tale to you now. But let me assure you that it is not delivered from beyond the bounds of Death – from the valley of Hell or the rosy clouds of Heaven (neither of which I wish to see for a very long time).

I will go back to the moment when the hatch first opened. There they were, the execution party: the corsair captain, the lantern-carrier, the first mate and another man, all staring down at me. It was the latter two who descended into the hold. The captain just stood there above us, lit by the golden light of the candle-lantern, glaring down into the gloom with his sword in his hand like an evil angel of vengeance, biding his time till he could carry out the threats he had so lovingly outlined.

I waited, despair closing in on me, more sure than ever that my encounter with the djinn in the night had been no more than a dream, the foolish fantasy of a condemned boy. With each step as they made their way down the ladder I felt what small hope I had had of rescue gradually snuffed out.

The pigtailed man and his helper reached the bottom of the steps. The pigtailed man was grinning from ear to ear, very pleased with himself. "You hoped captain would save you. Well, he won't. He has decreed the rope for you!" he leered. "How we will enjoy to see you dance on air!"

He took the fateful keys from his belt, and bent and released first my feet, then my hands from the iron shackles. Who ever would have thought I'd be sorry to lose my iron cuffs?

I stood, and found my knees were trembling so badly I thought I might fall. But that would be shameful. If this was my time to die I would do so with some dignity. I would not cry or beg for mercy – I knew I would receive none – and I would not crumple to the ground. I imagined Da and Mam watching me from wherever the dead go and steeled myself.

The other man, a brawny fellow I'd seen given the heavy-lifting jobs on the deck – the barrels and hawser, the anchor chain – now took me in his iron grip. The pigtailed man stepped in close. "Was bad fall I took. Your fault. Time for you to feel some my pain." And he drew back his fist, then slammed it into my stomach.

The agony was immense. I gasped and writhed and not even the big man could stop me plunging face first to the ground. Down I went into the darkness, into the bilge-water and filth, and at once there was pandemonium.

"Shame on you, you bastard!"

"Hitting a defenceless boy!"

"You cowardly brute!"

"You damned bully!"

All my fellow captives started shouting, making a great hullabaloo that echoed around the enclosed timbers of the hold till it sounded as if an entire demon army was trapped in there.

Retching with pain, I looked up to see the pigtailed man take something from his belt. There was a sharp crack, followed by a cry; then the whip fell again. Now the big man was reaching blindly for me. His hands came closer and closer; then suddenly something seized me by the ankles and hauled me out of his reach. I could not see who had done this. It did not seem to be the man I had been sitting beside, for he was staring at the corsairs and seemed unaware of me. This being the case, I crawled around behind him, reckoning that though it was likely to save me only for a moment, it was still one more moment alive.

But I had reckoned without the djinns.

A few seconds later there was a stirring in the darkness before me, as if something was on fire and the air was rippling with a heat I could not feel. Quickly, it appeared to take on the ghostly forms of four human figures, which almost as soon as they had formed flowed together into a single entity, gaining substance all the while. The djinns were swift and illicit as they went about their business of deception: even the flames in their eyes were extinguished. And then abruptly where there had been only darkness, there was a shape lying in the bilges where I had but lately been: a Jude-shaped boy with shaggy dark hair, dressed as I had been dressed – still *was* dressed – as perfect a copy of me as you could imagine.

Almost as soon as it appeared, the big man seemed to spot it. Grasping the figure, he hauled it upright, and as he did so, I saw my own face gazing back at me.

I very nearly cried out then, and the djinn-Jude's face immediately mirrored my own in a silent cry. I stared and stared. There is nothing quite so strange in all the world as seeing yourself as others see you, to be outside your body, while still inside, looking out. I found myself marvelling at the detail they had noticed and recreated. There was the bruise on the left cheek that the corsair chief had left there when he dealt me the stinging blow to the head when I asked about little Alice. There was the rip in my shirt and the ragged cuff. And the figure appeared as solid as I did myself. There was no transparency to the simulacrum, nor did the corsairs' hands pass through it as they seized upon it triumphantly.

As they neared the foot of the ladder, the djinn-Jude wriggled and writhed in his captors' hands, giving them a difficult job of getting him on the ladder. In my own voice, though with a slightly odd accent, he cried out, "No! No! I won't go up there! I will not go to my own death! May Allah preserve me!" As they struggled with him, a small dark shape came flying through the darkness and latched itself on to the pigtailed man, who whirled around, accusing the djinn-boy of kicking him.

168

"If I were free I would kick you a thousand more times!" cried the djinn-Jude, and the captives below applauded his spirit.

Their whistles and catcalls masked the sound of a certain ring of keys hitting the ground. It seemed the first mate had not noticed their loss, for he gave the captive boy another hard blow for good measure and the djinn-Jude at last sagged into the brawny man's hands as if submitting to his fate. The big man threw the copy of me over one shoulder as easily as a sack of meal (maybe this version of me was lighter than I was, I reasoned, though if it was, it did not seem to alert his suspicion) and up the ladder he went, closely followed by the pigtailed man.

As the light from the candle-lantern caught the djinn-Jude's face, it tipped me a wink.

A moment later the hatch came crashing down, and we were left in pitch darkness.

A moment after that, I sensed something making its way slowly towards me. I could make out a few pale splotches amongst the darkness: apparently unattached shapes, like anti-shadows, white on black. And it clanked as it moved, as if by some mechanical means.

What new strangeness was this? At last the black and white patches resolved themselves into a small black and white cat with its tail up and its rear end facing me, stepping precariously from beam to beam as it struggled to stay out of the bilge-water. It appeared to be dragging something heavy which sporadically caught and hindered its progress.

"Byasen!"

The very same, he mumbled. *Take these wretched keys from me before I slip and drown in this stinking place!*

I bent and took the keys from his mouth, and rubbed my hand across his small silky head and he butted my knee and purred and purred.

You attacked that fearsome pirate! You stole the keys! Byasen, you're so brave!

I know.

When I came to the first man, he could not believe it. He held his hands in the air in front of him and stared at them. "Have you really freed poor Daniel Tamblyn? Bless you, boy!" Then he reached out and felt me to make sure I was real. "Is it you, lad? How can that be?"

I assured him it was.

"Then who was that poor boy? And how did you get the keys?"

These were very good questions and I was about to try to explain, but at that moment I espied a fiery glow in the middle of the hold and out of this glow materialized a dozen figures. They looked very much like the crew of the ship in their tunics and breeches, their dark skin and shaved heads, and in the swift and nimble way they moved. In the midst of them towered one with silver earrings, and golden bracelets which encircled its arms. I recognized the being with whom I had made the bargain in the night.

Zaafran! You have come!

Zaafran bowed his head in acknowledgement. *We are*

here to keep our part of the bargain, but there is no time to
waste.

I turned to the captives. "Do not be afraid — they are here to help us. They are not demons, but creatures called djinns. They come from Morocco, just like the pirates, but they are our friends, and they're going to help us!"

Several of the captives looked from one to another. I could see them quite clearly, lit by the fiery light of the djinns. They looked puzzled, but not alarmed.

"What is the boy wittering about — djinns and suchlike?" asked a thin, grey-haired woman.

"Poor lad," said Susan. "It's all enough to turn anyone's wits."

It was only then that I realized they could not see what I could see.

We only appear to those by whom we wish to be seen, said Zaafran. *It's a knack the People of the Flame have always had. We find it very useful in difficult situations such as this one. If we appear to these folk, they will only panic, and we do not have the time for that. Quickly now, Jude, unlock them and we will make our move while the corsairs are busy with your execution.*

I held up the keys, and rattled them, and that soon made the captives forget their difficult questions.

"The keys!" cried Daniel Tamblyn.

"Jude! You're a hero!" shouted a brawny fellow with yellow hair.

I moved amongst them, opening their shackles and

171

removing the bars that held them in place, and they fairly danced to be set free, waving their arms and kicking their legs about. Daniel Tamblyn grabbed the woman called Susan and spun her around and around.

"We're free!"

Another woman enfolded me in her arms and pressed me against her capacious bosom. "I don't know how you've done it, lad, but I love you for it."

Even Jack Two gave me a hug; and the foreign man taken with the others off the Scilly Isle muttered a gruff "Thank you" and clapped me on the shoulder.

"Now we have to get out of here," I said. "And then we shall take the ship!"

A great cheer roared through the hold. The captives were captive no more.

22

A BATTLE

How did we get out of the hold? you may well ask. The corsairs had locked the hatch behind them, and the djinns, for all their magic and trickery, could not touch the iron latches. And yet, it opened. . .

There came the grating sound of the bars being shot back, and then the heavy wooden lid slowly opened. Two heads peered down. Two heads with hair as fine and pale as thistledown.

"Agnes!" I cried. "And Alice, too! But how. . .?"

"Your cat brought us!" Alice declared cheerfully. "He's been keeping me company ever since I was ill, but he only spoke to me for the first time today – isn't that funny?"

She looked down. Beside her stood a third figure, small and piebald, with glowing amber eyes in which I was sure I saw flames flicker and dance. They regarded me with amusement.

Byasen?

The chet sounded cross as he replied. *You know perfectly well I am down here.* He burrowed up my shirt and stuck his head out through the opening. *Can't you tell the difference between your own friend and a djinn?*

I looked again at the third figure. It looked exactly like Byasen: but then it didn't, for as I watched it became wispy and dissipated, before reforming as a tall, dark-eyed girl.

My name is Yasmin, said the djinn. *Come up quickly, while they are occupied above-deck.*

"Thank you!" I said aloud. "Thank you for coming."

I was not sure for whom it was meant – the girls or the djinn – but all three of them responded with a smile.

Up through the companionways we ran – girls and boys, men and women, the djinns and one small cat – arming ourselves with whatever we could find on the way. In the Place of Food, we took the ladles and some knives, and Susan and the grey-haired lady helped themselves to a couple of huge frying pans. In the Place of Guns we found two muskets and some powder, three of the curved swords and some cudgels. It wasn't much against the crew of a ship as big as the *Baraka*, but it would have to do. Besides, we had surprise on our side.

I crept up the ladder leading to the top deck with my soup ladle over my shoulder and stuck my head up cautiously. A large group of sailors was gathered up on the foredeck, watching something. My eyes focused upon a small, limp figure hanging from the yardarm of the mast, swinging in the cool breeze off the sea.

It is not something I will ever forget, seeing myself hanging there, crick-necked and lifeless. For a moment I felt

I was that boy, and felt my blood run hot, then cold. My knees begin to shake.

It is only a copy of you, Byasen reminded me. *Though a very good one.*

Go on! said Zaafran, flowing past me. *If you want to take the ship you must act now. We cannot do the fighting for you. Our physical presence is not yet sufficiently strong, especially in the sunlight. But we will do what we can.*

I did not know what he meant by this, but there was no time to ask. I led the captives up on deck with our makeshift weapons. The attack was something that should have started silently, but after days imprisoned in the dark and filth of the hold, the captives were not in the mood for stealth. As soon as they caught sight of the enemy they started to roar and curse. Up to the forecastle they raged, ready for battle.

A moment later I heard a loud bang and saw a puff of smoke and one of the Barbarymen spinning to the ground, blood pouring between his fingers from the musket-shot wound that had taken part of his arm away. After that it was all chaos and noise.

A woman ran pell-mell into the fray, braining a sailor with her frying pan and running to take on another. One of the foreign captives dived at the brawny man who had carried the djinn-Jude out of the hold and pinned him against the gunwale, all his fury channelled through his merciless fists. I saw Jack Two whirling a long wooden stave about him, hitting one sailor over the head and another across the back so that he went flying. But the corsairs were not men to be defeated easily. Despite their surprise at seeing the prisoners free and armed, they were rallying quickly, drawing their curved blades and daggers, and howling war cries in their foreign tongue.

A thin bald-headed man came towards me brandishing a wicked little knife. I dealt him such a thump with the long-handled soup ladle that I took myself by surprise. The blow laid him low and the aftershock rumbled up into the bones of my arm so that I almost dropped my weapon. At that moment I suddenly found myself confronted by the pigtailed man. His eyes became round. His mouth hung open in shock. "But we hang you!" he said in amazement. His gaze slid to the yardarm and the frayed rope that still hung from it, then back to me. Then he screamed, "If you not dead yet, you will be soon!" And he came at me with his flashing blade.

It whistled towards me like white death, and I felt the air from its passage blow against my skin. I ducked desperately and my feet went out from under me, for the deck was slick with blood, and I found myself flat on my back, utterly defenceless. The first mate grinned. "Now I have you!" he cried, and brought the sword up to stab down at me.

Something punctured my chest painfully and then a small black missile launched itself from me towards the pirate and hit him squarely in the groin with its hard little bullet-head. It was the chet!

The man cried out as all the air went out of him and his scimitar buried itself in the deck a foot away from me.

Byasen! You saved me!

Tit for tat, the cat grinned back at me. *But that's enough of that!*

I saw him weave between the forest of feet and vanish and could not blame him. What could one small cat do in such a melee? Indeed, what could one boy do? I had lost my weapon, and now the first mate had recovered himself and was coming towards me with a dagger in his hand and murder in his eyes.

I scrambled to my feet and tried to get away, but the deck was dense with people fighting hand to hand and I could not forge a passage. Instead, I turned and grabbed at the hilt of the curved sword, but the strike had been hard: it was stuck fast in the planks.

On he came. "Why fight it, boy? You already dead!"

Something whooshed past me, blowing my hair into my eyes. When I brushed it away again, I saw the golden, smoky figure of Zaafran flow into the shape of a great lion, his jaws wide and scarlet, headed right for the first mate's throat.

The pigtailed man screamed and dropped his dagger. In his wake came a tide of djinns: three huge grey wolves with eyes of fire; a goat-headed creature with small, leathery wings; a dragon, breathing flame; an enormous serpent, its hood fanned out around its long, flat head, its fangs bared to strike; a hound and a mountain cat; a vast, sharp-toothed rabbit; a monstrous spider and a giant warrior wielding a sword of fire.

It seemed only the corsairs could see this magical army: for it was only the Barbarymen who shrieked and put their arms up to protect themselves, or simply ran in terror. I saw two men climb up on to the gunwales of the ship and hurl themselves overboard pursued by a gigantic eagle with its wings spread and its talons bared to rake and claw. Was it only me who saw that it made no shadow as it passed?

The captives, taking advantage of their opponents' sudden and inexplicable retreat, bore down on them with increased fury, and soon had them penned in the bow.

The pirate chief was the last to give up his sword. He stared wildly around at his crew. "Cowards! Craven cowards!" he shouted at them — or at least this is what Zaafran told me later, for of course he shouted at his men in their own language. "Can you not see that these are just djinns? They are not real: look! My sword goes right through them!"

And indeed, as he swung his scimitar the goat-headed creature in front of him simply melted away before my eyes.

"We cannot bear the touch of iron," Zaafran said, appearing beside me. "Not even when it is tempered into good Toledo steel. We are very careful to avoid their weapons; but Ashim is very wily. He will be fine."

But by then it was too late. In the heat of battle, and seized by fear, the corsairs had not realized their advantage. Now they were being pressed by flesh-and-blood enemies threatening them with their own weapons; though it was the women wielding frying pans who seemed to terrify them most — more, even, than the djinns. They cowered away, covering their heads with their hands. The women wanted to keep on beating them even after they had surrendered. Cornish women are like that: they will harbour a grudge for life.

But they'll also remember a good deed done. After Daniel Tamblyn and some of the men had at last disarmed the corsair captain and herded him and his crew below decks and chained them in the slave-rows in the hold, promising them proper Cornish justice when they reached Penzance, Susan and the grey-haired woman, who told me her name was Sally Bolitho, made a great fuss of me and the chet.

"You're a proper little hero, Jude," Sally said, "and we'll make sure everyone knows it as soon as we get back home."

Home.

The word struck a melancholy note. Truly, I had no home — in Cornwall, or anywhere else in the world. Mam and Da were both dead and buried, and all the reasons why I had walked away from our little cottage, and got myself tricked by wicked Uncle Momo, came flooding back at that moment. I thought about being an orphan, and about grim Aunt Purity and the workhouse, and Bodmin. That was what awaited me back in Cornwall. And yet all around me, other people were happy and celebrating our great victory.

I smiled weakly and accepted their hugs and their praise

and their promises of good home cooking – of pasties and pilchard pie, figgie hobbin and heavy cake and saffron buns.

As the once-captive fishermen and foreign sailors took charge of the good ship *Baraka* and set a course back to Cornwall, I found myself wondering what on earth I was going to do once I got there.

23

GOLD

That night the djinns came to me in the captain's cabin. There were a dozen of them, led by Zaafran. They crammed themselves into the small room in all their various forms. Thankfully, since it was not in their best interests to terrify me and the chet out of our wits as they had with the crew, they made a great effort to adopt what I took to be their usual appearance, which means very nearly human. Apart from the fiery light in their eyes, their transparency and their unnerving shape-shifting. But every so often it was as if their concentration failed and I would catch a glimpse of a cloven-hoofed foot, a goat's head or a pair of cat's ears, which just as suddenly as they had appeared melted away again. I could tell that Byasen saw these momentary transformations too, for occasionally his nose and whiskers would twitch with curiosity, and maybe just a touch of anxiety.

Zaafran sat cross-legged in his big white turban and his long white robe, smiling expectantly. "So, Jude. You are free and the ship is in the hands of your fellow captives. Now it is time to fulfil your part of the bargain."

I looked around, picking out amongst the djinns the girl Yasmin, who had brought Agnes and Alice to our aid. Beside her were two boys who bore a remarkable resemblance to her. I recognized one of them as the boy I had seen in the cabin on my first night here. She saw me looking at them and said, "These are my younger brothers, Nouh and Candal."

I must have looked surprised, for she laughed. "We djinns have families too, you know. We are just like people, in all respects but one. Some of us are benevolent and some of us are not. We choose our path in life, like you do. We can decide whether to be good, or evil. We can weigh our actions and make our choices. We eat and we sleep, we marry and have children, we love one another and hate one another and have friends and foes, dreams and ambitions, just like you."

"It is true," said Zaafran, seeing the disbelief on my face. "And everyone you see here is a part of my family." He took the hand of the female djinn beside him, a striking woman who wore her long black hair in intricate braids and whose big hoop earrings glittered as she moved her head to nod to me. "This is my wife Mimouna. And these —" he indicated three handsome fellows in blue robes decorated with elaborate swirls of yellow embroidery"— are my cousins Merra, Rihan and Ashim. We are all members of the Banou No'man clan. Until now we have been doomed to be eternal wanderers. But we hope that condition is going to change."

He leaned forward, his eyes quite literally blazing, and suddenly an eagle's beak appeared in the middle of his face, sharp and yellow and ready to rend and tear.

I must have recoiled, for he recovered himself swiftly and sat back, folding hands that were now human again. "We have a dream, Jude — a dream that all of us share; a dream that we believe you can help us to accomplish, if you will just fetch us the gold which is hidden here!"

Ah, the gold. Now we came to the nub of things. It seemed djinns and people were not unalike after all.

I got to my feet, and the chet jumped down from the chart table where he had been sitting and followed me to the far side of the cabin. I rolled back the bright Turkey carpet which hid the corsair captain's wooden chest. It was with the utmost effort that I managed to haul it up out of its hiding place, for there was no one who could help me, none who could touch the iron with which the chest was bound. The iron did not stop my hands from burning with their desperate gold-itch, either, and soon the proximity of all that precious metal made the burning spread all over my body. If someone had offered me a bath in the sea at that moment, I might very well have taken if, even though I could not swim.

At last the chest sat on the floor between me and the djinns. They all stared at it avidly, their gazes round and fiery.

Beneath the box lay a big iron key. I picked this up and

fitted it in the iron lock and turned it. Then I pushed open the lid.

The cabin was filled by a collective gasp of wonder and desire. But I looked at all the shiny yellow stuff inside, at the jewels and precious stones, at the ingots and the bars and the coins – pistoles and ducats, thalers and doubloons, crusados and pieces of eight – stamped with the heads of a hundred different kings from the world over, and then I closed my eyes.

Gold is a curse, Mam had said, and I believed her.

But the djinns had no such doubts. I could sense their shapes flowing all around me, pressing close. They had no real physical presence and yet I felt them. I felt their hands on my shoulders and my back as they pressed against me, craning to stare at the chest of gold.

"Take it out! Take it out of the box," Zaafran urged me, his voice deep and raspy.

"Tell me why," I said. "Tell me why it is you want the gold so badly, and then I will take it out of the box."

Zaafran tore his gaze away from the chest with the greatest of difficulty. "If I tell you, you will know our weakness."

"If you do not tell me, I will not give you the gold."

"You made a promise."

I had, it was true. But even so, I shivered. It was the way they were all staring at the gold, as if they wanted to devour it. I swear, one or two even dribbled with greed; and as I watched, their shapes flowed and changed, then changed again. Faces and hands and skin gave way to scales and feathers and fur; claws and talons and beaks; hooves and whiskers and fangs. Then I was really afraid.

I snapped the lid shut again, and heard the groan that rumbled around me. I knew, though, that while the gold was still inside the iron-bound chest, there was nothing they could do to me. They wanted the gold, and only I could give it to them.

"Promise me that you won't hurt me or Byasen. Or any of the others," I said desperately.

"We will not hurt you, I swear."

"Then tell me what will happen when I give you the gold." I folded my arms and tried to look immovable, but it was as much to stop myself from trembling, or showing them that I did.

Zaafran stretched hands that showed talons growing from his fingers towards the chest as if to warm them at a fire, then pulled them away quickly, as if he had been burned. "The iron," he moaned. "Please, Jude, take the beautiful gold out of the box, away from the cruel, cold iron."

"Tell me."

The djinn sighed, and it was as if a wind blew through the cabin. I saw the fur on Byasen's head stir and ruffle. His ears twitched with annoyance.

"Without the touch of gold we are like ghosts of ourselves," Zaafran said huskily. "Formless, meaningless and lost. We drift like clouds, like mist – like smoke – and barely know one another. Without gold, life is chill and lonely, for we – the Banou No'man – are cursed, cursed to wander for ever, without form and without a home. It is for this reason that they call us the Goldseekers."

I shuddered. It seemed I was much like a djinn myself.

"All we want," Zaafran went on, "is to become more like you; more human. We want to make a life for ourselves, to stop wandering, to put down roots. Put a little gold in my hand and you will see what I mean."

I hesitated. Then I opened the chest, drew out a handful of heavy yellow coins and placed them on the djinn's upturned palm.

For a moment, I thought they would fall right through his grasp, for I could see the bright colours of the Turkey rug through his hand as if through a mist. Then his fingers closed on the coins and I watched as the colour of the gold transferred itself to him and spread through him like a fire.

He reached out over the box, iron and all, and clasped my shoulder, and the touch of him was warm and real. He grinned at me and his eyes were bold and bright. But no longer were they frightening pits of flame, but warm and dark and sparkling with golden lights.

"But where is the gold I gave you?" I cried in some awe, for I could see that his hand was now empty.

"It is part of me now," Zaafran said. "I have absorbed it. Like food."

Byasen now stepped past the chest of gold and butted his head against the djinn and Zaafran reached down and stroked his head, and the chet purred and purred and purred.

"Ah, Byasen," the djinn said, "that is better, is it not?"

Give them the gold, the chet told me. *It will do far less harm in the world in the hands of djinns than in the hands of men.*

He was right. Suddenly, I knew it. Gold is a curse, Mam had said; but it seemed that gold could also lift a curse, and if that were the case then perhaps there was a balance in the world that even Mam – the wisest woman I ever knew – had known nothing about.

"The gold is yours," I said to Zaafran. I moved towards the iron-bound chest, but the djinn caught hold of me.

"You're a good boy, Jude, and you will be a good man."

Releasing me, he took off one of the armbands he wore and held it out to me. It was silver in colour and very heavy, as wide as a thumb's length and etched all over with complicated patterns. I had never seen anything quite like it, for the bracelets my mother wore were thin and delicate, and I had never before seen a man wear jewellery.

"Put it on," Zaafran urged. "As a symbol of our kinship. And wear a sleeve over it so that others don't see it. If you have need of me at any time, take it off and rub it and say my name and I will come to you, wherever you are. For you are now my brother, and I am in your debt."

I drew the armband over my hand and up my forearm, but still it lay loose and heavy, so that if I dropped my arm it would rattle down into full view and clatter around my wrist. But as I pushed it further, past the elbow, it suddenly began to squeeze, like a hand wrapped around the muscle there, and when I looked it sat snug against my skin as it had against the djinn's, as if it had been made for me.

"Thank you," I said, though I was not sure what any of it meant.

Then I bent and took a good hold of the corsair captain's wooden chest and with a huge heave, tipped its gleaming, glittering contents all over the Turkey rug.

I watched Zaafran descend on it like a vulture at a feast. I saw him pick up a huge gold pin with a ruby head and plunge it into his turban; then he fell upon the gold with an appetite. I picked up Byasen, stepping quickly away before I was lost in the stampede as the djinns swarmed forward, and went to seek more human company.

24

THE HOMECOMING

Two days later we came within sight of land. A great jagged tooth of rock stuck up out of the surface of the sea with a froth of white waves crashing all around it. The foreign sailors crossed themselves at the sight of such a danger in the middle of the ocean, but Daniel Tamblyn, who had been steering the *Baraka*, laughed. "That's the Steeple," he said. "Though the French call it the *Loup* – the Wolf Rock. The wolf that keeps enemies from our door!"

Now that the erstwhile captives had their enemies locked in the hold, they were already elaborating the stories they would tell of their trials and triumphs once we put into Penzance harbour. The more they elaborated, the smaller became my part in their release. Agnes was indignant on my behalf, but I just smiled.

"I'm happy enough not to be mentioned," I told her as we stood at the bow, watching the waves separate before us, parting the sea in twain like a comb through hair. "It's probably for the best."

She frowned. "What do you mean, Jude? Don't you want to be a hero?"

I laughed. I was no hero. Heroes were brave and steadfast at all times. Heroes did not dread the sight of their homeland fast approaching, for fear of what lay in store for them there. Heroes did not break out into a cold sweat at the mention of the word "Bodmin", or the memory of what they had left behind. I had some plans forming in my head, but they were hazy yet and I was not ready to share them.

"What will you do when you get back?" I asked her instead, and watched as her features pinched in on themselves, as if she held her feelings in check behind the muscles of her pale face. I remembered, abruptly, what she had told me back on St Michael's Mount: how their mother had sold her and Alice in the market to Uncle Momo, and cursed myself for asking such a stupid question.

"I don't know," she said in a voice barely above a whisper. "I don't know. I've been trying not to think about it."

"I'm sorry," I said, and I was.

"It's not me I'm worried about," she went on after a long moment. "It's Alice. If it were just me it would be all right. I can do lots of things to earn my keep – I can wash and sew clothes and cook, and milk a cow and take honey from a comb without upsetting the bees. I can churn butter and make cheese and look after hens; but Alice is too little to work, and it would be a rare employer to have the kindness of heart to take in two mouths to feed when only one is earning."

I could see her point. "You can do a lot more than I can," I grinned, trying to make light of things. "I can't really do anything! Mam once said I'd be the richest man in Cornwall, but she never said how, exactly, that would come about!"

Agnes's pale face broke into a smile, and it was as if the sun had come up behind her eyes. "Your mam must have loved you very much, Jude, to say such a thing."

I felt a sharp pain inside, and had to turn away.

And now I saw Alice coming to find us, climbing up the stairway to the foredeck with Byasen in her arms. The pair of them seemed almost inseparable, I thought, as if they shared a single "range", in the chet's parlance. For a moment I felt a pang of jealousy, but the look on the child's face was one of such bliss as she came up towards us with the cat cuddled close that it soon dissipated, like morning fog being burned away by the sun.

Along the south Cornish coast we sailed, past the unmistakable tawny granite promontories of Land's End, marching one after another like soldiers into the sea, then past the cliffs of Chair Ladder and the Terrier's Tooth. As we continued, people pointed out the landmarks, their voices warm with happy memory and the knowledge that soon they would be back amongst loved ones in that familiar landscape that only a day or so before they had thought never to see again.

"There's the Logan Rock, that I climbed as a lad!" cried the yellow-haired man.

"And there's Porth Curnow, where my pa taught me to swim!" cried someone else, as we passed a dip in the gorse-carpeted cliffs where the tumbles of sandy granite gave way to a great sweep of silver sand fringed with white surf.

As we passed the tiny cove of Penberth, Jack Six shouted suddenly, "I can see my sister's cottage!" He screwed up his eyes and shaded them with one hand. "Michael's boat's out, laying lobster pots, no doubt, but isn't that Jocko, their wolfhound, nosing for crabs in the rock pools? Ah, it'll be a handsome Sunday dinner for me when I get home!"

I knew that if I still had my lodestone and held it out in front of me on its thong it would spin and rock and twitch towards the north – over the hump of the cliffs and the rocky spine of the land beyond. Over the moors, all heathery and buzzing with bees, lay our cottage and beyond that Da's sett, and somewhere the two bodies of my parents, now cold in the earth. I shivered.

We passed the stone mine at Nansmornow and the dark cedars of Kelynack Point and then it was Jack Four's turn to cry out at the sight of the village of Mousehole. The Spaniards had sailed into this cove in my great-grandda's day and burned the place to the ground, but the Cornish are resilient folk, and now it was rebuilt, as snug and secure as you could wish, tucked safely away behind its harbour wall. It was hard to imagine those angry survivors of the defeated Armada storming through those quiet streets with murder and destruction in their minds. Jack was grinning from ear to ear at the sight of his home, but my mood had turned even darker, for there was St Clement's Isle, lying offshore. The last time I had seen it was on the voyage out, over the shoulder of Malik the corsair captain, as he ordered poor Jack Three tossed overboard like unwanted ballast.

As we rounded the gentle green slopes of Penlee Head, the town of Penzance came into view with the sun shining on its sturdy granite houses and the steeple of St Mary's Church, from which Barbary raiders had stolen all those people nearly forty years ago. I thought of the pirates confined in the hold of the *Baraka* and found a grim satisfaction in the thought that we had in some small way avenged their fate. These pirates, at least, would not be stealing Cornish men and women again.

We sailed into the wide, welcoming arms of Mount's Bay and in the afternoon sun the Mount looked as placid as could be, the castle on its summit like the castle in which a prince and princess might live happily ever after at the end of a fairy tale. But this was not a fairy tale, and I had no castle to return to.

As we passed the island I scanned it for any sign of Uncle Momo and Mary, and the little cottage where they had kept us prisoner, but there was nothing to be seen on the seaward side but rocks covered in seabirds and seals basking in the sun. It did not look for one moment like the roost of the blackest of villains.

Suddenly there came a barrage of shouts and cries which

drew my attention away from my search of the Mount. A flotilla of vessels of all sorts and sizes was converging upon us. There were fishing boats and skiffs, luggers and ketches and little rowing boats, all jammed with folk waving muskets and staves, looking as fearsome as the Cornish can. Lessons had been learned from the Spanish invasion and the Barbary raid. They were ready to do battle with whoever it was who had the gall to sail unbidden into their waters.

Suddenly I realized what had drawn their ire. At the top of the mainmast fluttered the pirates' flag – a dark green pennant showing an armed upraised with a curved sword in its hand and three crescent moons besides. I realized that in our heady delight at taking back the ship we had forgotten to take it down. One of the foreign sailors looked where I looked and then stuck his thumb up to me and went running off across the deck, then climbed up the ratlines as nimbly as a monkey, arriving at the top in moments. Taking the knife he carried between his teeth, he cut the flag down and threw it into the air. For a moment the wind took it and spooled it out against the bright blue sky, rippling like a great serpent. Then it folded in on itself and plummeted towards the surface of the shining sea and was swallowed by the waves.

A cheer went up from the new crew of the *Baraka*. All this noise must have attracted the attention of the djinns, for I saw Zaafran's head appear in the hatchway leading up to the foredeck. Quickly, I ran down to him. "We are coming in to port. I do not think it would be wise for people to see you and your family, or they may take you for corsairs too. I would not wish them to hang you."

Zaafran grinned at me, his solid bulk filling the hatch. "I'd like to see them try! But you may be right: perhaps, to avoid misunderstandings, we will stay out of sight." He ducked back down below.

Now the fishermen of Penzance and Newlyn, seeing the pirates' flag gone and the foreign ship apparently crewed by smiling folk, including some women and children, stopped waving their weapons in such a threatening fashion and began to look puzzled.

Jack Five climbed up on to the gunwale and waved wildly at one of the approaching boats. "Da! Da, it's me!"

A grizzled-looking man in the bow of the leading ketch stared so hard it seemed as if his eyes might pop right out of his head. Hollowing his hands around his mouth, he cried back, "Ollie? Is that really you?"

And then the pair of them were both laughing and crying at one and the same time, and that pretty much set the tone from that moment on.

Word soon spread from one boat to the next; then to the shore. Everywhere people were shouting and laughing, and in a little while a hymn rose up from the quay in praise for our return. All the little boats trailed in around us, like seagulls crowding around a fishing vessel at the end of the day, hoping for the heads and guts from the catch, and suddenly the clamour and rejoicing of it all was too much for me.

I fled belowdecks.

"Zaafran!"

No reply. I ran to the captain's cabin and flung open the door. The cabin was in disorder, the chart table and chair overturned, the carpets ripped up and the wooden chest tipped over. And everything it had contained was gone — even the silver and the jewels. And so were the djinns. So much for that, I thought. So much for kinship and brotherhood. They had disappeared. As I turned to leave, I thought I heard an echo of laughter hanging in the air, as if they were hiding, playing a game with me, and I turned back, half expecting to catch a glimpse of a tail or a wing, a laughing eye or a clawed hand. But the cabin was empty. No one appeared.

Dejected and bereft, I made my way up on deck again. Already, the longboats had been launched and the first loads of rescued captives were on their way to the shore, among them the yellow-haired man and Sally Bolitho. The rest were all grouped around the rail, waving and shouting and waiting their turn to board the boats.

I hung back and watched the celebrations as family members pressed through the throngs on the quay to gather their loved ones in their arms, and friends and neighbours patted them on the back and shook their hands. Such a jolly mass of mankind. Who would not want to be a part of it?

I felt the promise of tears sting the backs of my eyes. What was I going to do? Now that it came to it, the grand plans I had been quietly hatching – of escape and riches and revenge – had vanished along with the djinns, and I was just a boy with no family.

The longboats plied their way back and forth, shuttling between the *Baraka* and the shore, and the group of people waiting to be shipped out grew smaller all the time. I caught sight of Agnes and Alice. They were also on the edge of the group, hanging back, along with the foreign sailors we had taken from the Scillies. All of us with no one to welcome them home. The emptied longboats were rowed back by volunteers and loaded up to the gills with eager folk again, and another, bigger, boat came with it. This one carried the town's constables and a group of armed men. They no doubt intended to take the corsairs to the jail, though where they would hold them all, I had no idea. The sight of them decided me: I would take my chances on the land. I did not want to be questioned about who I was and how old I was and where I lived by the constables.

Agnes, Alice and I were in the next to last boat to leave the *Baraka*. All the way towards the shore I scanned the crowds, hoping I would not see there the beadle and the parish officers come to fetch me away to Bodmin, for during the course of the day, this idea had set its teeth in me like some snarling, fearsome dog that has got a good hold and will not let go.

In we came to Penzance harbour, until I could make out the individual stones in its old sea wall, the rosettes of orange lichen growing upon the granite, the line of weed that showed the high-water mark. Then my gaze fell upon a woman in the crowd. Our eyes locked. Framed by a starched white cap above her plain black dress and plain white collar, her face was stiff and stern. Stiffer and sterner than I had remembered it, even in my worst nightmares.

It was my Aunt Purity.

25

BYASEN'S DANCE

Yes, there she was, the miserable old Bible-basher, waiting for me on the quay.

If I had known how to swim, I would have pitched myself out of the longboat and into the sea right then and there. But I was more scared of drowning even than I was of Aunt Purity, which is saying something.

I watched in dread as she made her way to the front of the crowd, never once taking her eyes off me.

"That boy is my nephew!" I heard her declare for the benefit of the gathering, her voice as shrill as the seagull's. "He'll be coming home with me to learn some proper Christian values. Gallivanting around the high seas with heathen pirates! I blame his poor dead mother for marrying beneath her, a ruffian of a man who spent his life scratching in the earth for riches while his wife was reduced to living the life of a peasant. The boy's not had a proper upbringing, never once been to church. Well, he shall come to live with Goodman Pengelly and myself and we shall instil the lessons of the Lord into him with proper Christian discipline."

"Is that your aunt?" asked Alice, her eyes as round as plates.

I nodded unhappily. "I'm afraid so."

"She seems . . . horrible."

"Alice, you should not speak ill of strangers," her sister admonished her.

"No, Agnes, Alice is quite right. That is my Aunt Purity and horrible is the kindest word I can think of for her."

The chet pushed his head up out of my shirt where he had taken refuge when we got into the boat. Byasen disliked the idea of falling in the sea even more than I. He took one look at Aunt Purity – at her stark clothing and her clawlike, pointing hand and hawk's beak of a nose – and burrowed deep down inside my shirt again.

I did not blame him. If there had been a giant sitting behind me whose shirt I might have climbed inside to hide myself, I would have done the same thing.

Closer we came and closer with each stroke of the oarsman's blades, and with each yard of water that we covered my aunt's voice got louder and shriller. She was at the top of the landing steps, making quite sure I could not escape her.

"I shall do my Christian duty!" she was crying. "It will be a hardship taking a savage creature into my house, but it is my duty."

Savage creature, said Byasen into my mind. *Does she mean me?*

I fear not, my friend. I believe she means me.

"Spare the rod, spoil the child, that's what I say. My sister was too soft-hearted by far, and in the image of her wild and ragged child you can see the result of such laxity."

As the boat scraped against the quayside, I held back with Agnes and Alice, letting the others in the boat disembark before me. At last there was no choice but to make the ascent of the steps.

At that moment, I wished I could shapeshift like the djinns. I'd have grown a roaring dragon's head, or turned into a lion or a great stamping elephant. Or better still, something with wings that would bear me away from this place. But I was just a boy with no home, and no magic, either. As I climbed the steps to the quay my legs felt unsteady, as if at any moment my knees would give way and drop me in the sea. But they carried me to the top, where a dark figure loomed over me.

"So there you are. What a dance you've led us on, disappearing like that! We searched the county for you after your ne'er-do-well father threw his life away down that wretched mine. From Helston to Hell's Mouth we searched to bring you back to the Lord's path. Much wasted time and effort, all to no avail." My aunt looked past my shoulder to Agnes and Alice. "Who are these two urchins?"

"They are friends of mine. They have no family but me now."

Aunt Purity pursed her mouth, deepening the lines etched all around it by her constant disapproval of the world. "Well, they will not be coming with you. We cannot take in every Dick and Harry, nor every Jane and Jill. Family is a duty: charity begins at home. It'll be the workhouse for them, no doubt," she said, reaching forward to take me by the ear.

At that moment there was a disturbance in my shirt and I felt Byasen's feet scrabbling against my chest. With a titanic effort he lurched out of the opening of the shirt, straight at Aunt Purity, feet splayed, hissing like a snake. She let go of me in an instant and shrieked in disgust.

"Agh! What is that – a rat? Shoo! Shoo! Get away from me, you filthy, flea-ridden thing!"

The chet landed neatly on the quayside, and there wove a clever, busy pattern between my aunt's feet as if he were dancing a gavotte, the way I had seen him do with the pigtailed man at the hatchway to the hold. For a moment Aunt Purity stood there, flapping her arms like some vast crow trying to propel itself into flight. Then she lost her balance and plummeted head first into the seaweedy waters of the harbour. The great splash she made wetted everyone in the vicinity. There was no need for me to cry *Help!* for all had seen her fall and at once two men jumped in after her.

I grabbed Agnes by the arm. "Let's get out of here!"

Together we dodged our way through the crowd, with the chet leading the way in delighted little leaps and bounds, crowing its triumph as we went.

Did you see that, Jude? Did you see what I did there? Filthy? Flea-ridden? Rat? I ask you. I think your aunt is either blind or extremely rude.

202

I grinned. *Maybe a bit of both.*

The throng parted before us, far too curious to find out whether Purity Pengelly would sink or swim to pay much attention to three children fleeing the scene. "Old witch!" I heard one woman say. "That will teach her for her preaching, ranting ways."

Heads down, we ran and dodged until there was some daylight between the throng of people. I turned to encourage Agnes and Alice, and as I did so ran slap bang into someone, who went down with a clatter and a cry, taking me down with them.

I hit the ground so fast I scarce knew I had fallen, let alone hurt myself. Scrambling upright, I came nose to nose with a familiar face. We stared at each other for a long moment.

"But you're dead!" I cried, at the same time as Jack Three grabbed me by the arms, exclaiming, "God's teeth, if it isn't Jack Seven!" And then, laughing at my utter bemusement, "Do I look like a ghost?"

I shook my head, but still I could not believe my eyes. "I saw the corsairs throw you overboard! How on earth did you not drown?"

"Just because you cannot swim does not mean that others can't."

"But your leg—"

"It hurt, but only afterwards. At the time I was too concerned to save myself to think of it. And I was in luck, for when I ran out of strength the tide carried me with it as far as St Clement's Isle, where I was washed up more dead than alive. Three Mousehole fishermen found me there and took me in. I lay like a corpse for two days, they tell me. I only came home just now on Farmer Jolly's cart and these crutches they made for me. And what's the first thing I see but the pirates' ship sailing into Mount's Bay? I thought they had come back to steal me again!"

We grinned at each other, and I felt as if a huge weight had been lifted from me.

"So what's that great ruckus going on over there?" he asked, indicating the quayside.

Aunt Purity was being hauled out of the harbour like a soaking-wet sack of spuds by Daniel Tamblyn and another man, and a great crowd was gathered all around to watch. In a moment she would be back on her feet and baying for my blood, of that I had not doubt. "Tell no one you saw us!" I made him promise.

"But won't you tell me what happened?"

"Another time!" I cried, as off we went at speed, and open-mouthed, he watched us go.

Down alleyways we plunged, out of sight of the harbour, along Wharfside, past the shipwright's and the fish market, the chandlery and the sailmaker's, up the hill, towards Chyandour and Long Rock. On the Market-Jew road there was a lot of passing traffic – drovers and carts, pony-traps and carriages – and I realized it must be market day.

A thought occurred to me. "Agnes, if we were to find

your mother, would you and Alice want to go home with her?"

The look she gave me was one of pure, round-eyed horror. "Jude, she sold us! She sold us to Uncle Momo, not caring what he did with us. Of course we would not want to go with her!"

"Even if I could make sure that there was enough money for your keep that she would never be tempted to do such a terrible thing again?"

"I never want to see her again!" cried Agnes.

So that was that, then. But it was a question I had had to ask. "All right, then," I said, my voice full of a confidence I did not feel. "I have another idea."

I thought something quickly at Byasen and he glanced at me curiously, then took off, running.

Alice burst into tears. "Byasen's running away!"

I knelt down in the roadway beside her. "He's doing something for us. He's being our spy."

This cheered her enough to stop her tears, but Agnes gave me a sharp look. "I won't be bought and sold by anyone. Not by Ma, nor Barbary pirates, nor you, Jude Lanyon!"

"I have no intention of selling you!" I cried.

"Well, I will not take a step further towards that accursed market until you tell me what it is you have in your head."

Girls. I swear they are as bad as cats, or djinns.

26

THE PRISONER RETURNS

Two hours later, as the sun was beginning to set, the chet and I were reunited, and we had a plan. Byasen perched on my shoulder, his little claws digging into my skin, while I shuffled slowly along the causeway in the growing dusk, heading for the looming dark shape of the Mount. Just one boy and his cat, alone in the twilight, suspended between day and night, land and sea, terror and triumph, or disaster.

We had left the crossing late: there had been a deal to see to before we left the mainland, and besides, we did not want to be seen, for we were on the track of prey.

By the time I made it across the shining path, the tide was lapping greedily at my ankles; looking back, I could see the sea had swallowed the causeway. There was no turning back now; our path was set, and now everyone on the Mount was held prisoner by the tide.

Once we were on solid ground, Byasen leapt down from my shoulder and rubbed his head against my leg. As we wound our way up through the darkening streets I looked

206

down at the tumble of granite cottages gathered around the tiny, gleaming harbour and thought how they looked like wanderers warming their hands at a fire, their windows like eyes glittering in the darkness. I recalled the last time I had made this journey, drawn on by Uncle Momo and his mackerel tabby cat, the promise of a home-made mutton pie and the welcoming embrace of "Goodwife Mary". Now, there was a distinct wintry nip in the air and I was a very different Jude to that naïve lad: or at least I told myself so to bolster up my spirits and quell my fears.

By the time we climbed the hill and rounded the headland above the village it was full night. I looked down into the bay. There was Penzance, a crescent of flickering lights in the distance, so far away that it might as well have been in another world. And there, the bobbing dark shape of the *Baraka*. Between us, the sea stretching silver and uncaring to the far horizon; above me, black rocks towered and below, far below, lay the low murmur of the waves.

There is something about approaching a place where you have been unhappy and afraid that stays with you for ever, no matter what your change in circumstances. It is as if a miasma swirls around you, enveloping you, cold and clammy, obscuring your vision, confusing your thoughts. As soon as I came within sight of the cottage where Uncle Momo had imprisoned me for all those long, fear-filled, sorrowful weeks, I could feel that fog pressing down upon me, turning my grand plans to stupid fancy, my certainties to vapour.

Whatever did I think I could do by being here — a lad of twelve with only his chet for company, against two determined brigands? Better to wait until daylight and let the authorities deal with Uncle Momo and Mary. Almost I turned back; but even as I thought about it, Byasen purred into my mind, *They'll be away before morning, gold and all. I can hear their thoughts. It is now or never.*

The little square of the cottage window glowed faintly in the gloom. Steeling myself, I pressed on, my heart thumping like a trapped bird. I could remember so well being inside, locked in the windowless back room, trapped and helpless, fearing the worst without being able to imagine the half of it. And as I thought of how they had imprisoned me there, along with all my fellow captives — all the Jacks and Agnes and Alice besides, with the intent to sell us into slavery — a great hatred rose up in me. And with it came a tide of anger so strong I could feel it beating against the granite of the cottage walls as fiercely as the waves on the rocks below the headland.

The anger gave me courage. I crept right up to the cottage, so close I could hear voices within. The little corner of tanned skin that served in place of window-glass that I had peeled back to peer out as Momo and Mary signalled to the corsair ship had not been repaired. Through that tiny chink I was able to peer inside. There they were, the two reprobates, sitting at the table, sifting through a small pile of belongings which were not their own. I caught sight of girls' clothing — a pinafore, a scarf, a petticoat — a rag doll, and a pile of coins. Their heads were bent over, intent: they did not see me. Behind them sat a girl and a boy, holding hands, looking scared out of their wits. The girl was older than the boy – maybe eight or nine; he, poor creature, was no more than six, with a mop of fair curls and blue eyes welling with tears which he was doing his manful best not to shed.

Had they been lured here in the same way I had with the promise of shelter and hot food? They did not look like ragged urchins. Or had they been sold to Momo like Alice and Agnes? Whichever it was, my heart went out to them. This wicked trade in human souls would cease this very night, I swore to myself. But I could not do it on my own.

I was just about to put my plan into action when the mackerel tabby cat, Amoush, leapt up on to the table between Uncle Momo and Mary. It lifted its green eyes to the window, to the small triangle of darkness at the corner that gave out on to the night, and stared right at me. Then he let out an ear-splitting yowl.

I just had time to see Uncle Momo rising from his chair and grabbing up his curved blade; then Byasen cried, *Run!* And we took to our heels.

Down the path towards the cove we ran, the chet and I, and the moon lit our way. Among the ruins of the cottages my fellow prisoners and I had spent our summer clearing of rubble, where I had let go of the great lintel that broke Jack Three's poor ankle, we stopped. And there, in the lee of one of the old stone walls, we took shelter and I looked back.

Three figures were clearly limned in the moonlight: Uncle Momo, Mary and the mackerel cat. Their eyes shone silver.

I shivered; then rolled up my sleeve.

Byasen and I looked at each other. Then I rubbed the silver armband that Zaafran had given me.

Nothing happened. I rubbed it again, harder, my hand powered by the jolt of terror that ran through me.

We stood there, the chet and I, alone in the darkness as our three pursuers came crashing down the path towards us. It had been a fool's errand, after all: a wild and absurd plan born out of all those heroes' tales spun to me by Old John and Abdellah, tales of glory, revenge and poetic justice in which the villains gain their just deserts in the end. Well, there would be no poetry in my ending, I thought, imagining the silvery light glancing off Uncle Momo's sharp blade as he brought it swishing towards my neck. I almost could feel its cold kiss on my skin, see the fountain of blood that would well up where once my head had sat, firmly attached by muscle and bone.

Hush your horrible thoughts! the chet told me. *Look, look there—*

I turned, to see a disturbance in the dark air behind me, like a gathering of smoke where there was no fire. It swirled and drew itself together and suddenly a pair of eyes was gazing at me out of the night sky!

I took a step backwards and fell down, banging my head

against the ruined wall in my surprise. But somehow, despite the pain and the shock, I did not cry out.

The eyes – black and shining with amusement, it seemed to me – blinked. Then a disembodied voice said into my mind, *You called?*

Zaafran?

The air glittered for a moment, affording me a view of a white turban above the black eyes. A giant ruby pin had been thrust through the folds of cloth to keep it in place: I recognized it from the hoard in the captain's chest.

I am here, little brother, as promised.

Do you see those men coming down the path?

The shape moved and the eyes and turban disappeared. From somewhere beyond the ruined wall I heard a laugh. *The men almost upon you with their cutlasses and knives in their hands and murder in their eyes? Those are the men who held you prisoner? Tell me, do you have an endless stream of enemies, Jude Lanyon?*

Quickly, I told him my plan, which seemed to amuse him even more. Then I stepped out from behind the wall.

Uncle Momo stopped in his tracks. He blinked and stared, then blinked again. "On my life, if it isn't Jack Seven. Come back to your Uncle Momo, have you? Too fond of Mary's delicious stew to stay with our pirate friends?" He took a pace forward. "I saw the ship. In the harbour. Knew something was afoot."

He peered past me into the darkness.

"What, not brought any friends with you?" Raising his

211

cutlass in a menacing fashion, he leered at me; then a movement caught his eye. Glancing down, he spied Byasen sitting beside me, his tail curled neatly around his feet, and his grin widened. "Just your little cat, eh? No constables or provosts? No soldiers or parish men? Now, that was foolish of you, lad."

"You'd better throw down your weapons," I said.

For a moment, he looked stunned. Then he turned to his companion. "Did you hear that, Mary? The boy wants us to disarm. What a card he is, eh? What a joker. Shall we do it, just to humour him? No? You're probably right, my old chum. You can never be too careful. A boy and a kitten might have tricks up their sleeves."

Mary threw his curved sword up in the air and caught it in his other hand. Then he snaked it about so that it gleamed wickedly in the moonlight. "Mahmoud never give up his blade."

Uncle Momo threw back his head and laughed and laughed. "Bravo, Mary: show the lad some tricks before we slit his throat, eh?"

He really was enjoying himself much too much, I thought. Perhaps it was time to make him laugh on the other side of his face.

Zaafran! I called.

There was no reply.

Uncle Momo took another step towards me.

Amoush snarled and hissed something which made Byasen lay his ears flat against his head.

Another step and I could see the scratches and nicks all over the blade of Momo's sword, he was so close.

Zaafran . . . now would be a good time!

The rising note of panic in my voice must have persuaded the djinn to act, for there followed a long beat of silence and then I heard foreign words and the air around me became turbulent, as if a great tempest were building around me, and one by one the djinns appeared, bursting out of the night air as if out from a curtain behind which they had been hiding all this time, which perhaps they had, for who knows what dimension such beings inhabit when we cannot see them in our own? One by one they coalesced, braiding and knitting the misty streamers of themselves into a single coherent shape.

And then, quite suddenly, there was a great gold dragon in the night air, its wings spread wide over my head, its fiery breath fuming through the darkness.

Momo's jaw dropped open. Mary began to scream; then he threw down his cutlass, turned and pelted back up the path towards the cottage, leaving the one-eyed man alone with the mackerel tabby.

The fur on Amoush's head spiked; then he yowled and yowled.

I thought he, too, would turn tail and run, but the mackerel cat had more backbone than Momo's partner. He stood four-square, his tail fluffed out in defiance, and glared at the dragon as if he could make it disappear by the sheer force of his will.

Then Uncle Momo did something very odd. Instead of screaming, or attacking the dragon, or running after Mary, he closed his one good eye and stood there, regarding the monster with his false eye so that the gold of the dragon was reflected in the depths of that black glass like a distant fire.

Then he laughed.

"Ha! A very fancy little illusion. Well done, Jack, my boy. You do have some friends in strange places. Well, you may have scared poor Mahmoud; but nothing gets past my little friend here. He's seen a deal of djinns in his time, has this cat. Came all the way from the exotic city of Marrakesh, didn't you, Amoush? All the way from the heart of Morocco. That's what his name means, you see – Amoush: it's the local Moroccan name for "cat". And djinns in Morocco are like mice in a hayrick: a deal of nuisance, he says, but not much more than that. Nothing to be frightened of."

He came forward, his cutlass held loosely by his side, and walked in a long, slow circle around me; around the dragon, with his good eye shut, peering with the glass eye as if he could actually see out of it. The djinn-dragon writhed and spun, breathing a fire that haloed the old man's head and beard, lighting the grey hair to flaming gold; but doing no damage at all. At last, he gave a low whistle. "I make that a round dozen of the beggars. Well, well. A dozen djinns, here on Cornish soil. That's quite a turn-up, isn't it? I won't ask where you found them, lad: they must

214

have come off Malik's ship; though how you managed to persuade them to perform their little party trick for you, I can't imagine."

Now he opened his other eye, and fixed me with it.

"Enough of the games, now, Jack Seven. I think it's time you accompanied me back to the house. Make your acquaintance again with my little back room. You'll find some new lads and lasses to make friends with there, not that you'll have a deal of time for socializing, for we're off on the first tide tomorrow morning. Decided a change of air was due; a nice change of scene. Got some friends in the Scillies we have, Mary and me, working hand in hand with the governor there. That'll be a nice safe nest to bed down in for a time, wait for the next Barbary ship to come through." He raised the cutlass. "Hop to it, my lad: wouldn't want to slice your ear off to make my point, now would I?"

As if they knew the game was up, the djinns drifted apart, the magnificent golden dragon coming apart at the seams.

Uncle Momo raised an eyebrow. "You see, Jack my lad, there's only two things in life you can trust." He waved his cutlass under my nose. "Good steel, and gold."

Something clicked in my head, something that made me grin. Perhaps I wasn't beaten yet. Perhaps there was still a chance. With a sudden bound, I took off running. *Come on, Byasen! Zaafran, Yasmin, Mimouna, everyone follow me!*

I ran across the uneven turf, studded with stones and

debris from the ruined cottages, miraculously not losing my footing, then plunged down the steep rocky path towards the cove. When I looked back over my shoulder I saw that Uncle Momo was in hot pursuit, and that Byasen and Amoush were already embroiled in a battle, hissing and spitting at each other like water spattering on a hot stove.

Where were the djinns? Had they abandoned me? If so, I was lost.

Zaafran?

There was no reply.

I did not have time to call again, even in my mind, for at that moment something whizzed past my ear, passing so close to my head that it took a hank of hair with it. It was the hair I saw first: a bizarre sight, floating down through the dark air like feathers. Well, I needed a haircut. A moment later I almost trod on the knife Uncle Momo had tossed, a wicked, curved narrow blade like the thinnest of new moons, with little patterns etched all over it. Without breaking stride, I scooped it up and ran on. If the djinns had given up on me and fled back into whatever dimension they had sprung from, I might at least try to defend myself for a short time.

But not for long. I thought of the curved sword Uncle Momo carried. He might have been an old man, but he was unnervingly spritely, and with the blade he had a much longer reach than I. But I was fleeter of foot, of that I was sure. And I would have to make that tell. On I ran. Fear and moonlight made me nimble.

Zaafran! I wailed again.

Nothing.

I came to the end of the jagged little path and jumped the last few feet to land with a crunch of shingle in the little cove. Over the weed-covered rocks I made my way, skidding and sliding on the slippery stuff.

And then suddenly I saw the djinns, in their human form, ahead of me. They were all together, floating and weaving around the entrance to Momo's cave in a hungry, frustrated fashion. I remembered the fat iron chain that had been set just inside the entrance, bolted into each side of the rocky inlet. It had not kept me out; but it was holding the djinns at bay. For a moment, I wondered if that had been Momo and Mary's intent; then I heard the sound of boots on the shingle, and that propelled me on.

With no time to spare for niceties, I pushed my way through the djinns. It was a strange sensation. I felt each of them as they parted around me like a fire that did not burn. I felt their personalities, each quite distinct – the angry confidence of Zaafran; the pride of Mimouna, the inquisitiveness of Yasmin and her brothers – and I caught their scents – rose petals, spices, charcoal and lemons – and then I was inside the freezing recess of the cave.

The iron chain would not budge, though I hauled and hauled on it. No time for that! I ducked beneath it and followed my twitching nose and itching hands. Bags of gold coins, up in an alcove hollowed painstakingly into the rock. I stuck the curved knife that Uncle Momo had thrown at me into the waistband of my trousers, and then I hauled down the bags of coin and hurled them one by one out of the cave. I never heard a one of them fall, which was strange. Gold plates I found, propped against the side. I spun them, flashing, through the dark air. Someone must have caught them, for again, they made no sound. Heavy ingots followed, bar after bar of them; then a pair of candlesticks.

At last I got hold of a big wooden chest and hauled it up with the superhuman strength of the truly frightened. By the time I had put the chest down, negotiated the iron chain, heaved it up again and come out of the cave, a strange scene was being played out on the strand.

Uncle Momo was on the rocks in front of the cave, his cutlass clutched so tightly that his knuckles showed white. Moonlight slicked off the glass eye, and the sweat that beaded his brow.

The djinns had him surrounded.

They were so solid from the gold they had eaten that when they moved the shingle crunched under their feet. Uncle Momo kept opening and shutting his good eye; but whatever the glass eye saw was not encouraging him. Then, he saw me. I seemed to offer him a less confusing target than the strange beings who encircled him, for he fixed his furious gaze on me.

"Damn you, Jack Seven! You've led me a merry dance!"

Then his eye dropped to the chest I held cradled in my arms.

"My gold! So that's why you came back to the Mount! I should have known. Despite all your fancy magic tricks you're just a wretched little thief! Put it down at once! I've worked hard for that gold, and I'll be damned if I'll let a little snip like you rob me of it!"

"Selling children as slaves, you call that work?" Fury rose in me, heating my words so that they came bubbling to the surface and spilled out of me in a flood. "That is the work of the damned, and damned you shall be. My mother always said that gold was a curse, and so you shall find it!"

And I let go the chest so that its contents spilled all over the rocks at my feet. At once the djinns began to laugh, a wild and eerie sound. The one nearest me — it was Mimouna, the wife of Zaafran, with her snaking black locks and swinging silver earrings — reached down and scooped a handful of coins up, then waved them in front of the old man.

Uncle Momo fairly danced on the spot, hopping from foot to foot, so great was his rage. "Those are mine! Put them down, you harlot!" And then he called her many other names that were even less polite, and which I cannot repeat.

She smiled at him then, a taunting, haunting smile. Then she opened her mouth wide so that all could see the flames within, and poured the coins down her throat. The gold coursed through her like a fire: you could see it spreading through her neck and arms.

I saw Momo's mouth drop open in confusion and fear, and then he ran at Mimouna with his curved sword raised.

He did not reach her, for Zaafran came at him like a force of nature. He wrenched the weapon out of his hands and sent it arcing into the sea. Then he encompassed the old man with his arms and squeezed until Momo cried for mercy.

"So, djinns are as harmless as mice, are they?" he cried, and his voice boomed around the little cove, echoing off the rocks like the angry roar of the sea in a storm.

At that moment, a black and white streak came flying through the air and landed at my feet. I looked down. "Byasen!"

The relief I felt to see my chet still alive, if not altogether whole, for a flap of one ear was bleeding profusely, was immense. He grinned, then took refuge behind me.

A second later the thing that was pursuing him cannoned into my legs, just I had cannoned into Jack Three. But a running Amoush did not carry as much weight or momentum as a running Jude Lanyon, so he did not bowl me over, but rebounded off me and went rolling, with an outraged screech, right into a rock pool.

I knelt down and hauled him out by the back of his neck. He hung, dripping, from my hand, as limp and compliant as a kitten. The water had plastered his fur close to his skin. He looked not so much like a mackerel tabby now but more like the fish for whom his striped coat was named.

27

THE TURN OF THE TIDE

The djinns and I marched Uncle Momo back up the rocky path to the cottage, where we found that the door had been locked against us. I saw something move at the window; then Mary's eye at the peeled-back corner, peering out.

When he saw Momo in the grip of the chief of the djinns in his human form, his eye went wide, and then disappeared.

A moment later his voice slipped out of the door, barely more than a whisper. "Don't let the demons near me, *min fadlek, sidi*. Please, please, Jack, sir, don't let them get me."

I handed the soaking-wet Amoush to Yasmin, took the little curved dagger out of my waistband and sliced the skin out of the window. Mary scuttled away from the door on his hands and knees. I stuck my arm through the window, reached around and turned the key in the lock. The door swung open.

"Drop your sword and lie face down, or I will send the djinns to come and fetch you," I ordered him.

His eyes skittered from me to Zaafran, then to Momo, sagging in the djinn's meaty arms, then to the others, and he threw his scimitar away from him and lay down on the floor. Stepping over him, I picked up the scimitar, took the keys from the table, unlocked the back room's door and peered in.

Uncle Momo had wasted no time in the few days that had passed since he had sold us to the corsairs. There were not just the girl and boy I had seen in there, but another four or five besides. The business in waifs and vagrants was clearly good.

"Do not be afraid," I said. "Come out: you are free now. My friends are outside. They may look a bit odd but they will do you no harm."

One by one they emerged from their prison: three girls and four boys. Their eyes widened when they saw Mary lying face down in the doorway, and beyond him Uncle Momo held prisoner by the djinns, but they were more curious than afraid, and out they came into the main room of the cottage. I found a coil of rope and Zaafran and I ushered Momo and Mary into the back room and made them sit on the floor. Then we tied them back to back using some special knots that the djinn knew.

"And that," he said, his fingers moving in a blur as he finished off our handiwork with an especially elaborate knot, "is a Turk's Head."

Momo pulled and struggled, but Zaafran had done his work well: he could barely move a muscle. I ran outside, took Amoush from Yasmin's hands and dropped him beside our two captives.

Byasen followed me in, looking very full of himself. He miaowed something at the mackerel cat, and the mackerel cat held his regard for a moment or two before dropping his head and looking aside, leaving the chet very satisfied with the exchange.

Then I locked the door and passed the keys to the oldest of the girls. "You hang on to these," I said to her. "The constables will be along shortly to take these bad men into custody."

I turned to the biggest of the boys. "What's your name?"

"Jack—" he began, before correcting himself. "Giles."

"Well, Giles, take this and guard the door." And I handed him Mary's scimitar.

He looked at me wonderingly, then at the sword. Then he reached out and took it, grinning, and at once began to flourish it, as if taking on invisible enemies.

"Don't wave it around," I told him sharply. "It's not a toy!"

I sounded just like my father. When had that happened, I wondered?

Byasen bumped his head against my legs. When I looked down, I saw that something was hanging from his mouth.

It was my lodestone, on its string. I scooped him up into my arms. "Are you trying to tell me something?"

As I took it from him the stone started to swing, crazily

at first, then with small, sure strokes, pointing north, always north. I looked at it sadly, then stowed it in my pocket.

"So what will you do now?" Zaafran asked me.

The tide would be turning in a couple of hours, bringing with it the constables to take Momo and Mary away to the gaol, to stand trial alongside the corsairs, if everything went to plan. My part in the capture was over. "I don't know," I said truthfully. I hadn't really thought about what would happen beyond this point; had hardly dared believe I could pull it off at all.

"Well, come with us," said Zaafran.

I followed the djinns back down to the little cove and there I went back into the cave and brought everything I found there out, beyond the iron. I laid it down on the rocks, and in minutes all the gold was gone: swallowed up by the djinns. But there was plenty of other treasure left when they had finished gorging themselves: bags of silver and copper coins, a long string of pearls and many jewels both in settings and as raw stones, and in these things they showed remarkably little interest.

I picked up the pearls and ran them through my fingers. They felt cool and silky against my skin and I thought how fine they would have looked draped around Mam's neck. I put that thought away and stashed the pearls in my pocket, along with a handful of stones and a bag of silver coins. Let the tide take the rest, I thought. Or the constables, when they came.

"Ready?" asked Zaafran.

"Ready for what?"

"I thought you said you were coming with us."

I blinked. "I thought you meant here, to the cove. For the gold."

"I meant home. With us."

Shocked, I stared at him. "Where are you going?"

"Back to Morocco. And then, who knows? I've heard there are cities in the Sahara in which the minarets are carved out of solid gold. Perhaps we are strong enough now to make that expedition. Or perhaps we'll just find an old palace in Fez and live there. But you are part of our family now, so come with us, Jude."

"How will you get there?"

He winked at me. "You'll see."

I thought about this for a long while, staring out to sea, his words rolling around my head like pebbles shaken in a bowl. They rattled and made plenty of noise, but signified little. Cities in the Sahara? Minarets carved of gold? A palace in Fez? The words themselves sounded exotic, promising adventure in far-off places. I was reminded of the tales of Old John and Abdellah the pirate: perhaps it would be my turn to bring tales to them and make their jaws drop and their eyes fairly pop out of their heads.

Besides, what was there for me here? I was twelve years old, and until I came into my majority as an orphan with no relatives I cared to live with, I was a candidate for the workhouse.

"I'll come with you," I said, and he grinned from ear to ear.

Mimouna, standing close by, came running towards me and hugged me and Yasmin danced around me, singing "Jude's coming with us, he's coming with us!" and making a complicated high-pitched trilling sound, her tongue shuttling back and forth in her mouth.

Soon all the djinns were dancing in a circle around me, whirling me around until I was dizzy. When at last they stopped I bent to catch my breath. Byasen was watching me from a distance, his eyes hooded. His expression was hard to read: I could not tell whether he was angry with me, or disappointed, or pleased.

I'm sorry, I said to him. *I did not ask what you wanted to do.*

He gazed at me steadily. *Where you go, I will go*, he said. *To the ends of the earth.*

I scooped him up, and he bumped his head against my cheek.

"Are you ready?" said Zaafran.

"There are one or two things I need to do first. Back on the mainland." I sat down on the rocks.

"What are you doing?"

"I'm waiting for the tide to turn, so that when it does we can walk down the other side of the island and cross the causeway."

The djinns burst into peels of laughter. "There's no need for that," said Zaafran, and in an instant he had transformed

226

himself into a huge bird. "Climb aboard," it said out of the side of its big yellow beak.

I held on tight as he beat his wings; but I was never once afraid. I held the lodestone in front of me and directed Zaafran and the rest of the djinns as we flew north. Over the silver sea we flew, just as the sun was coming up over the east of the bay. And there we passed the constables' launch, filled to the gunwales with armed men, heading for the island and thence to the cottage, with Jacks One and Three as their guides, to arrest Uncle Momo and Mary and bring the captive children back home.

We passed over the sleeping town of Market-Jew: up over Gulval and the ancient hill fort of Castle an Dinas where I first had met Momo; over the moors I had crossed with Byasen and my pack; over Watch Hill and all the way to Kenidjack. As we passed over my parents' cottage, I felt a lump in my throat at the sight of the weeds that had grown up around the door and taken over the kitchen-garden in the space of time I had been away. I noticed that a fence had been broken down by some cows that had escaped from nearby fields. But the beehives were still there, and I could just make out some bees buzzing cheerfully around them, as if they had decided to come home. In the sunny spot on the side of the hill was my mother's crocus patch. Tiny violet, white, and yellow heads were just beginning to surface and I had to blink back tears at the thought of how they would not be harvested this year.

One day I will return, I vowed then. One day I will come back and make gold flow again from both the hives and the flowers, in the form of honey and saffron.

The djinns set us down at the top of the lane and Byasen and I walked from there to the Scobles' farm. I waited till I saw Farmer Scoble go off into the fields with his dogs at his heels, and then I slipped across the yard with my chet behind me, and tapped on the door.

Mrs Scoble answered, looking sleepy and dishevelled. When she saw me she rubbed her eyes. "So it is you, Jude! I half thought I'd imagined you yesterday at the market." She ran a hand through her hair. "Come in, lad, have some breakfast." She ushered me inside her warm, fragrant kitchen. Bread was baking: she must have been up all night.

"Are they safe? Are they here?"

"The girls?" She smiled broadly. "Bless their hearts, yes, they're here. But they're fast asleep. Worn out, they are, after everything they've been through, especially the little one, who looks just like my poor lost Beth." A wistful look came over for a moment, before she was recalled to herself. "Shall I wake them, Jude? Do you need to talk to them?"

I shook my head. "No, don't. I just brought something for them. And for you." And I emptied my pockets out on to the table.

Mrs Scoble stared round-eyed at the pearls and the jewels. Then she stared at me, and I saw the sudden doubt in her face. "Whatever is all this, Jude? Have you been robbing folk?"

"No, I swear it. Not I." Others did the robbing, I thought; and though their gains had been ill-gotten it seemed only right that the most needy should now have the benefit of their wicked deeds. "I want you to take it, Ma Scoble. Take it for the care of the girls: make sure they have all the things they need in life. And wear the pearls yourself, at Christmas, and on feast days, promise me you will do that."

She nodded, bemused. "But what about you, Jude? What will you do?"

"I'm going a-travelling, Mrs Scoble. For a while. Will you look after Mam and Da's cottage for me, till I return and can legally claim it as my own? Will you ask Agnes and Alice to tend the garden, and take care of the bees?"

Her face broke into a huge smile. "Of course I will, Jude. Nothing would please me more." She hesitated. "But where are you going?"

I took the lodestone from my pocket and let it hang from its thong till it began to oscillate. "On the upswing it shows where north lies; but on the backswing it must show the south. That's where I'm going. A long way south."

An hour later a square-rigged polacca sailed silently out of Penzance harbour, heading south. It was the good ship *Baraka*, otherwise known as the *Good Fortune*, and it was manned by a most curious crew. If you looked closely, you would have been able to make out aboard her a dozen or more figures, some in dresses, some in tunics; others in far

229

stranger guises. A tall, white-turbaned man tended the ship's wheel; a dark-eyed girl had wrapped herself around the bowsprit like a living figurehead; men with eagles' wings trimmed the sails. And up in the crow's nest at the top of the mainmast with the wind blowing back the shaggy hair of the one and the fur of the other, sat a nut-brown boy with a wide silver bracelet on one arm and an etched silver dagger at his belt, and a small black and white cat.

They were off to the ends of the earth.